Diablo – The New Girl

Gabi Adam

Diablo –
The New Girl

Copyright © Gabi Adam 2008
The plot and names of the characters are entirely fictional.
Original title: DIABOLO – Die Neue

Cover photo: © Bob Langrish
Cover layout: Stabenfeldt A/S
Translated by Barclay House Publishing
Typeset by Roberta L. Melzl
Editor: Bobbie Chase
Printed in Germany, 2008

ISBN: 978-1-933343-97-6

Stabenfeldt, Inc.
457 North Main Street
Danbury, CT 06811
www.pony4kids.com

Available exclusively through PONY.

*For all those who believe their dreams
really can come true.*

Chapter 1

"I'm sure glad this winter is almost over," fourteen-year-old Ricki Sulai said to her friends Lillian Bates, Cathy Sutherland, and Kevin Thomas as she glanced out the stable window. "I was beginning to think I'd never see green grass again!"

"Yeah," agreed Kevin. "The cold and the snow have lasted a long time. But when you look outside today, it's hard to imagine that only two weeks ago everything was all white."

It seemed as though winter had just been blown away. The sun shone in the steely blue sky, tiny buds were becoming visible on the branches of the trees, and the crocuses appeared as colorful dots in the still rather faded green of the Sulais' lawn. The returning birds made a loud, cheerful chirping sound as they sailed lightly through the air.

"Fabulous!" Lillian sighed as she secured the girth around the belly of her white horse, Doc Holliday. "Holly, stop filling yourself up with air! I can hardly get the buckle into the first hole!"

Cathy made a face. "He's not doing that on purpose. I think he's just put on too much winter fat, like Rashid."

"Hmmm. Our horses aren't the only ones who've put on some winter fat. Look at me," Ricki added, giving her hips a rueful glance.

"Oh, you're fine. As long as you can haul your rear end into the saddle, you have nothing to worry about," teased Kevin.

"You think so?"

"Yeah, of course I do." The boy looked at his girlfriend tenderly.

"Do you know how long I've been waiting for this kind of weather?" said Ricki. "Now at least we can go riding without having to put on a thousand layers under our jackets and wearing gloves."

"We're a long way from T-shirt time, Ricki, but I don't want to seem ungrateful. The sun is really trying hard. Let's give this ride a shot. Are you guys ready? Can we get going?" Cathy looked at the others.

"Yeah!"

"Ready at the starting gate!"

"You bet!"

"Well, what are we waiting for?"

One by one, the friends led their horses outside the stable. Then they tightened the girths and mounted.

"Where do we want to ride?" Kevin asked as he sat astride his roan, Sharazan.

"Let's go visit Carlotta at Mercy Ranch," Cathy suggested, secretly hoping she'd run into her boyfriend, Hal, who often helped out at the ranch.

"How about Western Stables?" Lillian asked, thinking of her boyfriend, Josh, who boarded his pinto horse, Cherish, there.

"Echo Lake!" Ricki burst out a second later. For her, the lake was an enchanted, mystical place. She and her friends had many wonderful, memorable adventures there.

Laughing, Kevin leaned back in his saddle. "Oh, girls! Here you go again! Can't you ever agree on anything?"

"Well, where do you want to go?" Cathy asked.

"Don't say the wrong thing, now," Lillian warned.

"Hey, don't threaten me," grinned the boy. "I'll join the majority, if there is one."

"You know, you really have a clever way of getting out of making any decisions. Okay, then let's think this over," Ricki suggested.

"Well, we were just at Echo Lake a few days ago," replied Cathy.

"That's true."

"And Josh isn't at Western Stables yet anyway," Lillian remembered, "so it wouldn't be that exciting a visit."

"That's true, too."

Cathy was really happy. "Yeah, so Mercy Ranch it is."

"Okay, you win. Let's visit Carlotta and, for your sake,

I hope you get to see your Romeo today." Ricki grinned, bending over so she could hug Diablo's neck from the saddle. "Anyway, it doesn't matter to me where we go. The main thing is, we're going," she continued. "When I think that we couldn't go riding these past few months because of the ice, I'm happy we're even sitting in the saddle again."

"Yeah, you're right about that." Cathy steered Rashid off the gravel path leading from the Sulais' stable and onto the edge of a strip of meadow. Then she loosened the reins and let him go.

"Hey, you guys, when do you think Carlotta will start construction on her indoor riding ring? Maybe this year?" Ricki asked.

"I have no idea, but that would be great! Then we could ride warm and dry next winter," Kevin said.

"Please, don't even mention next winter," groaned Lillian. "I want to start thinking about summer, sun, and fun!"

"Hey, guys." Ricki had an idea. "Wouldn't it be great if we all could spend a few days at Highland Farms Estate again this summer?"

"Wow, that would be awesome!" Kevin agreed. "Maybe we should see if Carlotta would be willing to put in a good word for us with Mrs. Highland."

Eleanor Highland, owner of Highland Farms Estate, was an old friend of Carlotta Mancini's and, thanks to Carlotta, their friend and benefactor, the kids had been lucky enough to spend a few days at the estate with their horses last summer.

It had been a very exciting time, one they would never

forget, but it had also been a wonderful experience meeting Gwendolyn, Mrs. Highland's teenage granddaughter. Ricki had stayed in contact with Gwen, and Gwen kept Ricki up-to-date on the progress of her little foal Golden Star, at whose birth Ricki had assisted.

"Well, I'd love to see Gwen again, too," Lillian reflected. "She's such a cool girl!"

"Yeah, just like her grandmother," laughed Cathy.

"Sometimes I think Mrs. Highland and Carlotta could be sisters. They're so similar – well, not in the way they look, but in the way they act," Kevin observed.

"Hey, did I show you guys the newest photos of Golden Star that Gwen e-mailed me last week?" Ricki asked.

"No, I haven't seen them," said Lillian.

"Then remind me when we get back home. The little guy has really grown. Well, he's almost three-quarters of a year old already," Ricki mused.

"Really?! It seems like we were at the estate just last month. Has it been nine months? Hard to believe."

"You'll be surprised by how he's turned out. If you didn't know it was Goldy, you wouldn't recognize him. Hey, how about a little gallop? I can tell Diablo's dying to see how fast he can go."

"Ha! I bet! Don't blame everything on your darling horse. Why don't you just admit that you've been dying to gallop for the last few weeks," grinned Lillian.

"It's awful when your friends know you so well." Ricki winked at her. "All right, I confess. I need a dreamy gallop

– it'll do me good!" she laughed. And after the four friends had shortened the reins a bit, they urged their horses to run.

I've missed this so much, Ricki thought, as Diablo's gait became wider and wider. *Is there anything more wonderful than a fantastic horseback ride?*

As she bent low over her horse's neck, Ricki's face was whipped by Diablo's long mane and the wind made her eyes tear. A feeling of uneasiness came over her. Was it joy she felt, as she listened to the regular beat of her horse's hooves, or was it a longing for the ride to never stop? Was it her love for Diablo, which seemed limitless to her, or the fear that something could happen to end all this?

It doesn't matter, Ricki thought to herself. *There are so many things I feel when I gallop across the meadow on Diablo... too much for me to sort out inside my head.*

"Hey, watch out, Ricki! There are deer over there!" Kevin's warning shout tore the girl from her thoughts.

She was just able to steer Diablo away at the last moment. "Thanks! I didn't see them at all," she responded, a little out of breath.

"That's what I thought," Kevin answered as he pulled Sharazan up alongside Diablo. "When you gallop on Diablo you don't see anything. You always seem to be miles away."

"Hmmm," responded Ricki. "It sure looks like it!"

"You know you have to pay attention when you're riding!" Lillian scolded. At sixteen she was the oldest in the group and she always felt a little responsible for the others.

10

"Yeah, yeah, I know, Lily! Don't make such a big deal out of it. Nothing happened."

"Thank heavens! But think about it the next time."

"Yes, Mommy," grinned Ricki, and stroked her horse across the top of his mane. "This young man is very careful to make sure that nothing happens to me."

"Let's hope so."

"Oh, Lily, stop it. It's not like I just started riding and didn't know that you have to keep your eyes open. It's just that today I was distracted by other things. I guess that's because this has been the first gallop we've been able to go on in weeks."

"Oh, darn it!" shouted Cathy. "Stop, everybody! Rashid just lost a shoe."

"Didn't you notice it was loose when you were picking out his hooves?"

"Yeah, but I thought it would hold long enough to get us to the ranch. I'll have to tell Carlotta to call the farrier and make an appointment. Sometimes I'm really glad that Carlotta owns Rashid and not me." The girl dismounted quickly, picked up the horseshoe and then checked her horse's hoof. "It's all right. There aren't any nails left."

"Then let's keep riding. It's not that far to the ranch."

The kids rode slowly and continued to talk about Highland Farms Estate.

"What did Gwen say in her last e-mail?" Lillian wanted to know. "Anything new?"

Ricki furrowed her eyebrows as she thought it over.

"No, not really, but she did say that people keep asking if it's possible to take longer riding vacations there, and her grandmother has reserved a few of the older mares for their use."

"They must be busy if they're accepting long-term guests now," responded Kevin. "I wonder if they'll even have room for us?"

"Maybe we could help out for a few days," Lillian suggested. "We can't expect to stay there for free every time."

"My parents would never pay for a riding vacation for me, as long as I have the opportunity to ride Rashid, and Carlotta's other horses, for free around here," Cathy added.

"My mother would probably feel the same way," Ricki replied. "But wouldn't it be absolutely awesome to spend some time there? And I would love to see Gwen again, especially since she couldn't come to my birthday party."

"Don't remind me of your birthday," groaned Cathy, who had had a riding accident that day.

"Hey, look! We're here already!" Kevin realized with astonishment. "The way here seemed so much shorter today."

"Seemed like that to me, too," agreed Ricki, nodding. This made Lillian break out laughing.

"Do you two ever disagree?"

Ricki and Kevin looked at each other.

"Nope!" replied the girl, while her boyfriend said, "Sometimes."

"Great! At least you cleared up that question for me!"

Happy and laughing, the kids went through the ranch gate and brought their horses to the front of the stable.

As soon as she spotted them, Carlotta came out of the house waving at them invitingly.

"I was hoping you all might come by today. It's such a great day, I figured nothing was going to keep you off your horses. Can you stay awhile?" asked Carlotta.

"Of course!"

"We always do!"

"What's happening?"

"Are you getting a load of hay?"

Carlotta limped over to Rashid on the crutch she always used, ever since she'd been hurt in a riding accident, and patted him lovingly on his neck. "No hay," she replied, "but I have an appointment at town hall later today, and you know I don't like to leave the ranch untended."

"Isn't Mom still here?" asked Kevin, whose mother was Carlotta's housekeeper.

"No. She had a doctor's appointment."

"What kind of doctor's appointment? She didn't say anything about it to me this morning."

Carlotta grinned. "Sons don't always have to know everything, do they? But don't worry, she just went to the dentist for a routine checkup."

Kevin grinned. "Oh, her dentures must be wobbly again."

"Kevin! You're impossible!"

"How come you have to go to the town hall?" asked Ricki.

Carlotta shrugged her shoulders. "I have no idea. A friendly lady who works for one of the town offices called me yesterday. She was very secretive. I hate it when people don't just say what they mean, but what can you do? I'll just have to go and listen to what they have to say. I imagine it's about some regulations having to do with the ranch, but it may be something to do with my plans to build a riding ring. By now, they've probably all heard about it, before I've even submitted my application for a permit."

"Oh, official stuff, huh?"

"You said it! Miles of red tape. So, how about it? Can you stay here until I get back?"

"Of course!"

Cathy hesitated. "Is Hal here?" she asked shyly.

Carlotta laughed. "At the moment, no, but I bet he'll show up in an hour or so."

The girl beamed. "Terrific! I was afraid I wasn't going to get to see him at all."

"I wish I had your problems! Okay. Bring your horses into the stable and then come on over to the house. Caroline baked an apple pie."

"Oh, Mom's apple pie is the best!" Kevin got a dreamy expression on his face just thinking about it.

"Oink, oink!" teased Ricki as the friends brought their horses into the guest stalls.

* * *

It was with mixed feelings that Cass Meyers entered the riding hall where she kept her horse, Ashanti. Her weekly riding class, which she dreaded, was starting in half an hour.

14

The seventeen-year-old had exhausted her complete repertoire of excuses to try to get out of going, but her mother, unaware that her daughter had developed a real fear of horses over the past few months, had insisted.

"I just don't understand you. You had to have Ashanti, but now that he belongs to you, your interest has just disappeared. You used to be at the stable every day and now I have to force you to go to your riding lesson. What's going on? You can't just own a horse and then not take care of him. Don't you have any sense of responsibility when it comes to Ashanti?" Mrs. Meyers held her daughter's riding boots directly in front of her face. "Get dressed and go to the stable. I am not going to allow you to neglect him."

"But I have so much homework!" Cass tried to convince her mother that she just didn't have the time to go riding.

"Your sudden diligence is admirable," Mrs. Meyers said, unmoved. "But I'm sure you'll have plenty of time for that after your riding lesson. How many times have you been to see Ashanti this week?"

Cass avoided her mother's look. "Twice," she said softly, and crossed her fingers behind her back. Her mother would kill her if she knew that it had been two weeks since she had visited her horse, and that she had played hooky at a girlfriend's house instead of going to her riding lesson.

"Twice is not a lot. A horse, like any animal, needs regular attention and exercise!"

"I know, but I just couldn't get there," Cass said, continuing her lies.

"Hmmm," Mrs. Meyers frowned. She sensed that her daughter wasn't telling the truth, but she didn't know what to make of it. "Don't you get along with Chad Cameron?"

Cass shivered just thinking about her riding instructor. She really couldn't stand him, even though his classes were very popular with the other riders.

"Well, yeah," the girl answered hesitantly.

Mrs. Meyers continued to search Cass's face for clues. "I think I'll go with you to your riding lesson today. I want to see what progress you're making with Ashanti."

The girl's eyes opened wide with alarm. "Oh, uh, I don't know," Cass stammered. "Maybe it would be better for you to come the next time."

But Mrs. Meyers had already reached for her coat. "Who knows if I'll have the time next week to come with you. No, no, I really want to see your lesson. Anyway, then I can give you a ride back in the car so you can be sure to have enough time for your homework."

Now, Cass walked slowly toward Ashanti's stall. At least she had been able to convince her mother to sit in the spectators' seats so she wouldn't see the fear on Cass's face, which she experienced every time she was near Ashanti.

"Hey, Cass! I haven't seen you for a long time. Where have you been? Ashanti is developing a case of stall fever," Chad Cameron called out when he saw the girl approaching.

"I was sick," she mumbled and walked past him with a bright red face.

"Well, I hope you're completely recovered. Ashanti is probably raring to go after not being ridden for so long," he laughed. Cass turned pale and groaned. The riding instructor's words hadn't exactly made her feel any better.

Nervously, Cass walked up to her horse's stall and had to swallow a few times before she could open the gate. Ashanti looked at her with huge eyes before he began moving his ears back and forth nervously and blowing air excitedly through his nostrils.

He sensed Cass's uncertainty, and within a few seconds it had transferred itself to him as well. With a sudden movement, he turned around and kicked out at Cass, and she was barely able to escape out of his range.

Her heart was thumping wildly and she asked herself once again how she was ever going to be able to manage saddling the horse.

I don't want to do this anymore, echoed inside of her. *I'm scared!*

"Come on, Cass, we're going to start in fifteen minutes," she heard Chad's voice a few feet away.

"I can't!"

"What? What do you mean, *you can't?*" Astonished, the riding instructor came over to her.

"He won't let me into the stall," said Cass softly, trying to suppress her tears.

"Oh, that's ridiculous. Here, let me." Determinedly Cameron pushed passed the girl and opened the gate to Ashanti's stall.

"Ashanti, come here!"

At the sound of the instructor's commanding tone, Ashanti jerked a little, but then he turned right around and allowed Cameron to grab his halter without a problem.

Grinning, the riding instructor led the horse out of the stall and then snapped the lead rope onto the ring in the corridor.

"I don't know what's bothering you," he said to Cass, shaking his head. "He's as gentle as a lamb. Maybe he's just mad at you because you haven't been here in a while. I've got to go check on the others. You can saddle him by yourself, can't you?"

Cass turned bright red. She felt like an idiot. She was ashamed of her fear and embarrassed that she hadn't even managed to get her horse out of the stall. Terrified, she looked at her watch. If only this riding lesson were over and she were back home.

Cass held her gaze downward as she led her horse nervously to the riding hall. She knew the other riders were watching her every move and probably asking themselves how often she was going to be unseated by Ashanti. It was true the elegant and fiery gray horse had thrown his rider in every one of the previous sessions. It was even worse for Cass that her mother was there today and would see her struggle with Ashanti. She had told her mother after each lesson that the horse was wonderful to ride. Cass would never have admitted that she just couldn't deal with the animal and that she was so afraid of him it was impossible for her to look forward to the riding lessons.

In the middle of the passage, she stopped Ashanti, and then, with trembling hands, she attempted to tighten the girth. But the horse angrily scraped his hoof in the dirt, and then began prancing around his rider.

"Stand still, darn it!" Cass shouted at her gray horse and pulled on the reins, causing Ashanti to roll his eyes in fear. With rash steps backward, he tried to relieve the painful pressure of the bit in his mouth.

"Stand still!" Desperately the girl pulled on the reins again, which made Ashanti rear up. Shocked, Cass let go of his reins and the animal ran off through the corridor and into the hall.

"Blast it, Cass, what the heck are you doing?" Chad Cameron's voice echoed angrily toward her across the arena. The other riders were busy trying to keep their animals calm and kept giving her angry looks. Every time she took part in a riding lesson, there was complete chaos because she just couldn't take charge of Ashanti.

"Would you mind trying to catch him?" Cameron asked. Cass needed a few seconds before she could make herself chase after the panicked horse.

"Ashanti... come... stop," she shouted, although she knew that he would just ignore her and that Cameron would have to go grab the reins that were trailing along the floor.

Baffled, Mrs. Meyers watched all this from her seat in the gallery. She just couldn't believe this was the "wonderful" horse her daughter had been so enthusiastic about.

She watched as Cameron brought the horse back to Cass

and held him while her daughter tightened the girth and anxiously mounted Ashanti.

Cass was totally tense. She held the reins too short and pressed her legs too tightly against the horse's flank in order to feel a little safe.

Ashanti reacted predictably to Cass's confusing directions. He threw his head back and took several jerking steps backward.

Instead of letting go of the reins a little and loosening the pressure from her legs, the girl pulled the reins even more tightly and changed her weight toward the front, holding on with her legs, gripped in panic. This completely unnerved Ashanti. He shook his head wildly and then reared up almost vertically.

"Oh, my!" Mrs. Meyers cried out softly, her hand flying to her mouth in dread; she imagined that the horse was going to fall over backward and onto Cass.

Instinctively, Cass leaned forward even more and hung onto Ashanti's neck so that she wouldn't slide out of the saddle.

The horse had barely gotten back down on all four legs when she heard Cameron yell.

"Loosen the reins, Cass! And sit up straight in the saddle! Stop pressing your legs against his body!" But before she could react, Ashanti's abrupt shake of his head had pulled the reins out of her hands and the horse bolted like a rocket. He bucked back and forth across the riding ring, trying to rid himself of his unwelcome rider.

Everything happened very quickly for Cass. She saw the outlines of the other horses and riders vaguely flying past her. After one and a half rounds of what seemed like a real rodeo ride, she was catapulted out of the saddle and landed on the sandy ground, shaken and winded. Ashanti was no longer stoppable.

Chad Cameron ran over to her quickly and knelt down beside her.

"Are you okay?" he asked, worried now, and as Cass rubbed the sand out of her face and nodded, he looked up at Mrs. Meyers, who had jumped up in fright, and gave her a thumbs-up, signaling that Cass was all right.

"She's okay!" he shouted, and then he immediately turned to the bolting horse.

Cameron tried to calm him down with a gentle voice so that he could catch him, but Ashanti was wild. He continued to buck and was prancing like a whirling dervish. He held his head between his legs and kept bucking and galloping at a crazy pace until his frenzy was stopped suddenly and cruelly. While in a gallop, one of his front legs had become entangled in the reins, and he slipped and fell to the ground. A loud crunching sound was heard.

Incredulous, Cass stared at her horse, which was trying in vain to get up again. Then he remained motionless on the ground. His breath was jagged and his eyes filled with fear.

The other riders had followed Ashanti's fall anxiously and now they looked back and forth at each other with horrified glances.

"No!" Chad Cameron said, his lips pressed together. He ran over to the gray horse and stroked his neck comfortingly. Meanwhile he looked down at the horse and breathed deeply.

Ashanti's front leg lay on the ground in an unnatural position. The broken bones shone through his wounded flesh.

Cameron bit his lips, looked over at Cass, and slowly shook his head before yelling up to the spectators, "Call the vet. He should come right away and... and he should bring... the stuff he needs with him."

Cass had heard Cameron's words as though in a trance, but she was incapable of moving, and certainly she could not go near her horse.

She had wished so hard in the last few weeks that she had never begged her parents to buy a horse, that she wouldn't have to ride him, but she had never wished for Ashanti to die because of her.

She had failed. She had overestimated her riding skills and refused to admit it. She hadn't exercised Ashanti because of her fear, she had neglected him, and now it was her fault that he had felt this urge to move about, that he had gotten twisted up in the reins, and was now waiting to die with a broken leg.

Tears streamed down Cass's cheeks.

If only she could at least sit down beside her horse. If only she could stroke him and tell him how sorry she was that this had happened, but it just wasn't possible. The shock of what she had experienced was too great and, she admitted with a heavy heart, she was much too cowardly to face the accusing look of her horse.

Almost in slow motion, Cass turned aside and slowly exited the riding hall with her head hanging and shoulders drooping. Her mother, who had left the spectators' gallery as soon as she knew her daughter was all right, wrapped her arms around her silently and led her out to the car where Cass let herself fall onto the seat, weeping silently. Mrs. Meyers went back into the riding hall as the vet drove up and stopped with screeching brakes in front of the building. She would never forget the scene as Ashanti breathed his last breath a few moments later.

* * *

Carlotta knocked on the door of the mayor's office and entered almost immediately. Four heads, which were bent over a large construction blueprint, flew up, annoyed that their discussion had been interrupted.

"I hope you're all having a wonderful day!" Carlotta had a disarming smile on her face. "I don't know how important your meeting is, but I don't have much free time. I've been waiting for about half an hour, although I had an appointment, which was made for me. I didn't even get to choose the time! So, either one of you tells me why I am here today, or I'm afraid I have to go. I have some rather important things to do, and don't have the time to pace back and forth in the hallway!"

Just then Mayor Otis Gates recognized Carlotta. He got up quickly and hurried toward her with a welcoming smile.

"Mrs. Mancini, please forgive me for making you wait. We just forgot the time here."

"As long as you don't forget the work, I'll forgive you. Hello, Mr. Mayor. Whatever you want to tell me right now, please say it quickly."

"Well, Mrs. Mancini, I don't think it's going to be that easy to explain so quickly. It's a complicated topic which we want to discuss with you properly, and – please, sit down first. My colleagues already know you, and this is Warren J. Pendleton, from the national realty company Living Dreams."

Mr. Pendleton stood up. Carlotta nodded pleasantly at the two civil servants, and then she looked sharply into Mr. Pendleton's eyes.

Uh-oh, she thought. *This guy could be trouble. I'll have to be careful!*

"It's nice to meet you, Mrs. Mancini," Mr. Pendleton said as smooth as silk, offering her his hand along with a phony smile. Carlotta plopped down on the chair held out for her and waved him aside.

"We'll see if I'm glad to have met you, Mr. Pendleton," she said pointedly. "All right, gentlemen, what's on your minds? How can an old lady be of help to you?"

The mayor exchanged a quick glance with his colleagues, and then he took a deep breath.

"Well, Mrs. Mancini, it's about the following ..."

* * *

"It seems to be taking Carlotta a lot longer at the town hall

24

than she thought," commented Kevin as he gazed at the rest of the apple pie with longing.

"Oh no, young man! You've already had two pieces! Don't you dare touch that, unless you want Sharazan to collapse under your colossal weight!" Ricki threatened jokingly. "Carlotta might like a piece when she gets back."

"Well, I could leave her one piece, but she won't want half a pie."

"Did I just hear someone mention pie?" Hal came in laughing, followed by Cheryl and Lena, two other Mercy Ranch volunteers.

"Apple pie? Fabulous! Give me some!" Hal was already grabbing a large piece for himself.

"I'm really glad to see you, too!" commented Cathy, a little annoyed at her boyfriend. "Admit it, if you had to decide between me and this pie, you'd choose the dessert!"

Hal had to be careful that he didn't choke, he was laughing so hard.

"Oh, Cathy, don't tell me you're jealous of a pie. What have I gotten myself into?" Before Cathy could give him an answer he wrapped his arms around her and gave her a hug. "I like pie, but you're even sweeter!"

"Did Caroline forget the sugar?" Cheryl winked at Lena, who gave Hal a dismissive look.

"You men and your flattery... it's unbearable. And women are so stupid – they always believe them!"

Ricki couldn't keep herself from giggling. After all,

everyone in the room knew Lena had secretly hoped that Hal would become her boyfriend. A few months ago, however, he'd started dating Cathy.

"Where's Carlotta?" asked Cheryl. "She's not in the stable, and I want to ask her if I can ride Sheila."

"She had to go to the town hall on some business matter. She's been gone a long time," answered Lillian.

"Town hall? Why?"

"We have no idea. She didn't know herself."

"Okay, now I know exactly as much as I knew before!" Cheryl laughed. "Well, I guess all we can do is wait until she gets back. I think I'll go out to the stable and groom Sheila so I can leave right away, assuming it's all right with Carlotta."

"Good idea. Let's groom the horses. They've been outside in the paddock all day and they're pretty dirty. How about you guys? Are you coming, too?" Hal looked at them all in anticipation.

"Of course!" Kevin and his friends got up right away. "We should have thought of that a long time ago."

Chapter 2

Otis Gates, who as mayor was also chairman of the town's building and zoning commission, was startled by the raucous, dismissive laugh with which Carlotta greeted his carefully prepared presentation. He wasn't accustomed to being addressed in what he thought was a rude manner. He was, at least in his own mind, an influential figure in town politics, worthy of respect, and even deference.

"You must be joking," Carlotta bristled, an unmistakable tone of contempt in her voice. "You can't really believe I'd sell Mercy Ranch just because this gentleman here and his real estate company want to – what is it they say? – 'develop' the property, build a huge golf resort, with tennis courts, fast-food joints... and parking lots! What's next? Gambling casinos? That's not development, it's blight! Let me be clear about this, Mr. ... Mr. ... what's your name again?"

"Pendleton, Warren J."

"Well, Mr. Warren J., you're going to have to find another piece of land to wreak your 'development' on, because you won't get mine!"

"But my dear Mrs. Mancini –" Gates began.

Carlotta cut him dead. "In the first place, I'm not *your* dear Mrs. Mancini, and, in the second, I believe I have stated my position with sufficient clarity as to make any further discussion about this matter futile!"

Gates tried to stay calm, but he was getting panicky. Thanks to this stubborn old woman, the lucrative real estate deal he'd been concocting these past few months was in danger of falling through. "But didn't you hear how much Mr. Pendleton is offering to buy you out for? You'd be a wealthy woman. You'd have the means to build another – even bigger, better equipped – ranch for horses in another location."

"Of course I heard the price. I may be old and crippled, but I'm not deaf yet, and my brain still works fairly well. So let me tell you something. I don't give a hoot for the offer, no matter how high he goes. The animals at the ranch have finally found a home, a shelter. Many of them were abused and mistreated their whole lives. They never knew where they belonged, but now they do, and I'm not going to put them through the trauma of relocation just to accommodate you or Mr. Warren J. or anybody else."

Carlotta, propelled by a full head of steam, turned to Mr. Pendleton and continued.

"What's the name of your development company? Living Dreams? Well, as the owner of a company with a name like that, it shouldn't be hard for you to grasp that my living dream is maintaining Mercy Ranch and looking after the ill and neglected animals it shelters. I am fulfilling that dream at last and I'm happy right here... and richer than any amount of money you could pay me!"

With the aid of her crutch, Carlotta got up, pushed her chair back, bent over the conference table, and with feigned politeness said, "Thank you, gentlemen, for your interest and your *valuable* time. Your offer is an attractive and generous one, but – and this will be my last word on the subject – I'm not interested. Now I must go back to the ranch, where I'm needed. Have a nice day." With that she straightened up and, with deliberate slowness, limped her way heavily to the door.

Gates, otherwise extremely polite, remained seated and stared at the door, which had closed behind the eccentric elderly lady. Inside his head a storm was raging. His dream of creating a tourist center that would attract paying visitors from all over the country, and thereby filling the town coffers, was in shreds.

"So, that was the sweet old, *reasonable* lady who you assured me would be so easy to talk, eh, Otis?" Pendleton leaned back in his chair. "She acted like a horse-crazy thirteen-year-old! I can't believe anyone could be so stupid as to reject an offer like this. Can't she do the math? She'll never get an offer like it again for that old

29

barn and the couple of acres of land around it!" Pendleton was red-faced with anger.

"You heard what she said," Otis replied softly. "For her, it seems there are more important values than material ones."

"Oh, come off it, Gates. In today's world, the only thing you can count on is money. And this sentimental old lady will realize that someday, when she no longer knows how she's going to get the money to pay for the animals' feed." Pendleton paused to regain his composure before he continued. "I've got to have another talk with her – just the two of us. I'm sure I can find a way to convince her of the wisdom of taking my offer."

Gates looked at him and just shook his head.

"You can call Mrs. Mancini until the battery on your cell phone dies. Knowing her as I do, and considering what she just told us, you won't get anywhere with her. I think we might as well forget about the golf course, much as I hate to."

* * *

After grooming all the horses at Mercy Ranch, Ricki and her friends sat leaning against the outside wall of the stable enjoying the sun. Soon it would be time to prepare the stalls for the night and feed the animals.

"Carlotta's been gone such a long time, I'm beginning to worry about her," Kevin said squinting in the bright sunlight.

"Maybe the mayor invited her to dinner," Ricki suggested.

"Or she met the man of her dreams and eloped," grinned Lillian.

"Carlotta would never run off without the horses," responded Cathy, her head leaning against Hal's shoulder.

"Hey, I think she must have heard you guys talking! I'm pretty sure that's her old jalopy I hear in the distance." Lena pointed to the road leading up to the ranch.

"Terrific, but it's almost too late to go riding now," Cheryl said, glancing at her wristwatch.

"Then go riding tomorrow."

"It's always tomorrow! Easy for you to say. You guys have your own horses."

"Oh, come on, Sheila is almost like having your own horse, isn't she?"

Cheryl made a face. "Yeah, but only almost."

Slowly, the kids got to their feet as Carlotta turned into the driveway and brought her vintage Mercedes jerkily to a stop.

"Hello, my dears! Everything okay?" She waved to them and then got out of her car somewhat awkwardly.

"We're fine. How about you? We were beginning to think you'd run away with your secret boyfriend," grinned Hal.

"Oh, where is he?" Carlotta glanced at the passenger seat. "Hmmm, it looks like I lost him somewhere along the way," she laughed. "Is there any coffee?"

"Of course."

"I hope you left me a piece of pie."

Kevin looked off into the distance and whistled.

"No answer is an answer." Carlotta leaned on Cathy's shoulder. "Well, come on in with me, everybody. I have to

31

tell you something. You'll never believe the offer that was just made to me!"

"The way you say that makes me think it must be something unethical," Lillian teased.

"Depends on how you look at it."

* * *

Cass, with dark circles under her eyes, walked aimlessly around her room like a zombie. Ever since Ashanti's death she'd had trouble sleeping, and her dreams – nightmares, really – always ended with the image of her beautiful, proud horse lying helpless on the floor of the riding ring just before he was put down. At the same time, she had to admit to herself that Ashanti's death brought with it a peculiar sense of relief, liberation. She wouldn't have to go riding anymore.

I'll never have to ride again! she thought. *I'll never be afraid again... never be responsible for causing the death of a horse again... never again!*

Meanwhile, downstairs in the living room, her parents were engaged in a serious conversation about their daughter's peculiar behavior.

"She seems to be suffering terribly from the loss of her horse," George Meyers said to his wife, Thea.

"I'm not so sure," she replied. "I saw for myself how uneasy she was with Ashanti. You should have seen how he acted with her. I almost died of fright!"

"So you think we bought the wrong horse for our daughter?"

Thea Meyers nodded.

"But she was so sure she only wanted *that* horse, wasn't she?"

"Yes, that's true, but I think she just couldn't handle him. At least that's the impression I got when I saw her with Ashanti."

George Meyers looked at his wife and announced, "Let's get her a new horse! A calm, obedient animal. One she'll be able to handle."

"Do you think this is the right time for that? Maybe we should –"

"The sooner she has a new horse, the sooner she'll get over Ashanti's death. And I even have one in mind!"

Thea looked at her husband questioningly.

"Pendleton is selling his daughter's horse because they're moving, and Cameron tells me that Rondo is a very gentle animal. I've already seen him," he winked at Thea. "And I'm sure Cass will like him too."

"Well, if you think so," Thea said cautiously, "but shouldn't you ask her first?"

Meyers shook his head forcefully. "No. We're going to buy Rondo and give him to Cass as a surprise!"

* * *

"Beth! Hurry up! The movers are here!" Mrs. Pendleton, carrying a large overflowing laundry basket, looked back over her shoulder at her fourteen-year-old daughter, who had picked up a small packing box of books and was listlessly trailing her mother at a distance.

In front of the old mansion in the best section of the

small town, three men were busily unloading furniture from a huge moving van and setting it on the lawn.

"Where would you like us to put this antique sideboard, Mrs. Pendleton?" a young man with an unruly mane of reddish brown hair called out from the front doorway. "Ground floor or upstairs?"

"That goes upstairs, the first room on the right, across from the row of windows!" the new woman of the house called out, and quickened her steps.

"Fabulous!" the mover grumbled to himself. "Why do the heaviest pieces always have to go upstairs?... Okay, ma'am!" he answered pleasantly. He hoped this day would be over soon and that a sizable tip would compensate for his aching back.

"Beth! Where are you? Can't you move a little faster? If you keep this up your room will never be ready."

"Yeah, Mom, coming," the daughter answered, bored. She hated the move to this hick town. She'd left all her friends behind. She hated this old house, as she thought back to the elegant house she'd grown up in. And she hated the shabby little room in which she was supposed to live, starting today.

If only she'd been able to bring her horse with her. But no! Her father had to sell Rondo to that obnoxious competitor Meyers, just because he had offered him more money than her dad had paid for the horse in the first place.

"Believe me, it's better for Rondo, too, if he stays in his familiar setting," her father had argued, although he knew

34

nothing about horses. Beth had decided not to talk to him ever again.

"We'll buy you a new horse in the new town," Mr. Pendleton had promised in an effort to make peace with his daughter again, as they left. Beth, however, wanted only one horse, and that was Rondo.

Sighing, she went up to her room. Although the sun was shining full force and lit up the room, it seemed even gloomier to her than the first time she had seen it.

She would never feel at home here; of that Beth was convinced. Why was her father so sure he could make a success of his real estate company in this backwater town? And why had he bought this old mansion in this hicksville, instead of renting a penthouse in the closest larger town?

"Hey, you, just wait until your room is all fixed up with your furniture and your pictures are hanging on the wall. You'll see. It will be really pretty. I'm sure you'll like it." Nancy Pendleton had instinctively known what her daughter was thinking and was trying to infuse Beth with her own optimism.

"Whatever," Beth responded abruptly, but then she tried to put a smile on her face. She knew that this move hadn't been easy for her mother either.

"Oh, come on! It's not that bad here."

"Oh, Mom, admit it, you don't like it here any more than I do. I want to go back! And I want Rondo back!"

Nancy Pendleton grimaced. Even though she wasn't a

rider herself, she'd grown attached to her daughter's horse and could understand Beth's feelings.

"You know, dear, when your father makes a deal he never goes back on it."

Beth snorted loudly.

"Yeah, of course. The great businessman!" In frustration she threw the box of books she'd been carrying to the ground, scattering them. "Why does he get to make all the decisions? Why does everything have to be his way?"

"Beth, now stop it!" Mrs. Pendleton frowned in annoyance. "You're not going to change the situation by having one fit after another. That's just the way your father is and you should have learned to live with it by now. And, besides, he has his good points as well."

"Yeah, great! I'm thrilled! Why do you always defend him?"

Nancy looked at her daughter, silent for the moment.

"I'm married to him, honey, have you forgotten that?" she said softly.

"But you're not happy with him! Mom, I –" Beth walked over to her mother and wrapped her arms around her.

"I *am* happy!"

"No you're not!"

"Yes, I am! Now, do something to make this room a little more inviting. I have to go back downstairs." Nancy freed herself from her daughter's hug and hurried down the stairs before Beth could see the tears forming.

You've never been happy, her daughter thought. *No*

matter how often you say it, I know it isn't true. No one can
be happy with that man!

* * *

"Are they crazy?" declared Lillian, shaking her head, after
Carlotta had told them about her conversation with the
building commission.

"That would be awful! A golf resort. We certainly don't
need that here!"

"Our wonderful riding paths would be ruined!"

The kids spoke wildly all at once, and Carlotta looked at
one after the other.

"You're right, but for me the most important consideration
is the well-being of my animals. That's why I rejected the
offer, which I have to admit was very generous."

Kevin grinned from ear to ear. "That's you, all right! I'll
bet you drove those bean counters insane when you said,
'No way, José'."

Carlotta laughed out loud. "I probably did," she said,
and winked. "But I didn't wait for their temper tantrums.
I got out of there immediately. I'm sure, however, this Mr.
Pendleton won't give up that easily. I got the impression
that he's used to getting whatever he wants!"

"Well, then, he's about to have a whole new experience.
He won't be able to budge you!" said Ricki.

"Granite is like foam rubber compared to Carlotta's hard
head!" added Lillian, confidently.

"Hah! If he knew how stubborn Carlotta is, he'd give
up voluntarily!"

"Oh, thanks a lot! Now I finally know what you think of me," laughed the owner of Mercy Ranch heartily before she got up. "I think it's time to get to work in the stalls. My retirees are probably hungry."

"Oh, no, I almost forgot!" Cathy slapped her hand on her forehead. "Rashid lost a horseshoe on the trail."

"Do you still have it?"

"Yes."

Carlotta nodded.

"Good, then I'll call the blacksmith this evening. I need him for Sheila, too."

"Okay, then my question's already answered," declared Cheryl.

"You're talking in riddles," responded Carlotta, as she walked toward the stalls.

"Well, I wanted to ask if I could ride Sheila today, or tomorrow, but if her hooves aren't okay, then I guess I don't need to ask."

"Oh, child, of course you can ride Sheila! I just want to take off her horseshoes for the spring so she can go barefoot."

"Oh, good! Thank you!" Cheryl beamed happily and could hardly wait to saddle her favorite horse. However, first the work in the stalls had to be done, Carlotta was always firm about that. And so, soon afterward, the girl was swinging a pitchfork industriously.

* * *

"I think we've done enough for today," said Nancy Pendleton, letting her eyes sweep contentedly around the room. "There's always tomorrow!"

Beth breathed a sigh of relief.

She and her mother had been carrying boxes from one room to the other for hours and had unpacked thousands of things, which she had put away as best she could, so they could be found easily when needed.

It was already late afternoon, and Beth, looking out of the window, discovered that her bike was standing in the shade of a tall birch tree in the yard.

"I think I'm going to look around the town a little," the girl decided.

"That's a good idea." Nancy smiled encouragingly at her daughter. "Find out where your school is. After all, you have to start there on Monday. Maybe you can discover a supermarket and a bakery as well."

"Okay." Beth dusted off her jeans and ran outside. While she was checking the air pressure in her tires, she had to admit to herself that at least this huge yard, which belonged to her new house, was wonderful.

A tall hedge surrounded the spacious lawn and blocked it from the street. There was even a small pond, with a few water lilies floating on top, and a small open garden shed, and various bushes that would probably bloom in the summertime.

Mom will like this. Beth sighed and stood up.

Without Rondo and her friends, she felt really lonely, in spite of all the beauty around her.

She got on her bike and rode out into the street.

Where should she go? She looked left and right, and then she decided to go right. Actually, it didn't matter which direction she went. After all, in the next few days, she was going to have to get to know the entire area around her new home.

Chapter 3

Mr. Meyers and Mr. Pendleton came to an agreement about the sale of Rondo very quickly. Once the deal was complete, George Meyers invited his wife and daughter to go for a car ride, but he was very secretive about the details.

"Do you know where we're going?" Cass asked her mother, curious, but Thea Meyers just smiled.

"Wait and see."

"You two are so mysterious today!"

"Yes, hon, that's the way it is when you want to surprise someone!" Her dad grinned, and turned off in the direction of the riding stable. He was so sure Cass would be excited about Rondo he didn't notice that his daughter was becoming more and more upset as soon as she realized where her father was headed.

Oblivious to his daughter's state of mind, he parked the car in the stable parking area. As he got out, he signaled for her to follow him. "Now then Cass, come with me!" he said, and walked ahead briskly, while Cass, who felt as if she was going to faint, leaned on her mother.

No, rang loudly in her head. *Please don't! Please don't let it be what I think it is!*

"This is Rondo. But you already know him, don't you?" asked Meyers when they were all standing in front of the gray Arabian gelding. "He belongs to you now," Cass's father said solemnly, opening the door to the stall.

Involuntarily, the girl stepped backward and bumped into Chad Cameron, who was standing behind her.

"Rondo resembles Ashanti in appearance only; in all other respects he's an extraordinarily gentle horse. So there's no reason to be afraid of him the way you were with Ashanti," he said softly. Thea listened closely.

"You knew that?" asked Cass weakly.

Cameron nodded. "It was obvious."

"Why didn't you tell us?" Thea asked her daughter, shaking her head. "You always said –"

"I just couldn't," Cass replied. "You'd have thought I was crazy. First I wanted the horse, and then I became afraid of him. I didn't think you'd believe me."

Mr. Meyers listened attentively. "Maybe we would have understood, but I'm sure you're going to be happier with Rondo. He's not temperamental or wild, is he, Chad?"

The riding instructor shook his head. "No. Absolutely not."

Cass stared at the gentle-looking Arabian, but then she shook her head.

"Please, don't be mad at me, but I don't want another horse. I don't want to ride anymore!" she burst out crying.

"You're not serious, are you?" George Meyers stared at his daughter, who nodded shyly.

"Oh, terrific!" Disappointed that his surprise gift had been rebuffed, he pushed the door of the stall shut and stomped outside without another word.

Sadly, Cass watched her father go. It wasn't as if she didn't know how much pleasure he had intended to give her with Rondo, but –

"Maybe you should sleep on it overnight," suggested Chad Cameron full of compassion. "I'm sure you and Rondo would make a great pair. Why not give him a chance to show you that not all horses are wild mustangs?"

"Yeah, maybe," Cass said softly, and she turned around and walked after her father with heavy steps, without even glancing at Rondo.

Thea looked at the riding instructor, completely at a loss.

"What now?" she asked hopelessly.

Cameron shrugged his shoulders as he stroked Rondo's forehead.

"We'll just have to wait and see what she decides to do, but I think at least she'll try.

* * *

This hick town really doesn't have much going for it, Beth thought to herself as she rode her bike through the quiet streets. Although she had discovered a movie theater, a tack shop, a coffee shop, various other stores, and a lovely landscaped park, she just couldn't find anything to like about her new town. She still missed her old familiar surroundings and was convinced that she would never be happy here.

Happy? she thought. *What does that mean, really?* And it wasn't the first time that she had had these thoughts.

She rode out of town, straight ahead on a narrow road, until she saw a lonely farm in the distance surrounded by several fenced-in paddocks. She stopped her bike, got off, and surveyed the scene.

At least the area is attractive. It seems ideal for rides through the countryside, Beth thought and then, almost immediately, she had to fight back the sadness that welled up inside her when she realized she would never ride along this trail with her beloved Rondo. Just the thought that he no longer belonged to her almost broke her heart. Not a day went by that she didn't think about Rondo and hope that he was doing okay.

* * *

Ricki and her friends were on their way back home from Mercy Ranch on their horses when they spotted a solitary bike rider, a teenage girl unfamiliar to them. She seemed to be lost in thought, or perhaps just lost.

"Hi!" Lillian greeted her warmly from atop Holli's back. "You seem to be looking for something, or maybe you're lost. Can we help you?"

"Hello," Beth responded with a shy smile. "I'm new here and I just wanted to find out where this road goes."

44

"Oh, how long have you been here?"

"We just arrived today."

"Oh, wow, then you probably wanted to escape all that moving stress, huh?" asked Ricki sympathetically, "You always feel as though you're just getting in the way on moving day. I know."

Beth laughed, and felt herself relax a little around the friendly teenagers. "You're right about that. By the way, you guys have really beautiful horses."

Cathy beamed and patted Rashid's muscular neck. "Thanks! Say, do you ride, too?"

Beth's expression turned hard immediately. "I used to ride, until recently, but now I don't have a horse anymore," she said sadly.

"Oh, that's really too bad," stammered Cathy, at a loss for words.

Beth turned away. "It's not just too bad," she said through clenched teeth. "It was unbelievably mean of my father! He sold Rondo when he decided to move here!"

Ricki exchanged a quick glance with her friends.

"He just did that? I mean, without even asking you?" she blurted out in disbelief.

Beth nodded sadly.

"That's really cruel!"

"It's more than cruel! I miss Rondo so much."

Ricki thought hard about what she could say to encourage this girl, who seemed really nice, but she couldn't think of anything, so she tried to change the subject quickly.

"Will you be going to school here?" she asked innocently.

"Yeah. I start the day after tomorrow. They put me in Ms. Murphy's class at the high school. With my luck, she's probably the worst teacher in the school!"

Beth made a comical face.

Kevin burst out laughing.

"You're going to be in the Murph's class? Fabulous! Welcome to the club! That means you'll be in our class. I guarantee that you will love her!" To show that he was lying, he held up his hands and crossed his fingers.

Even Beth had to laugh at that. "She can't be any worse than our Mr. Blanton. Boy, am I glad to be rid of him!"

"Well, see you. We have to be going so our horses can get something to eat. See you in school, okay?"

Beth nodded.

"Sure, of course. Hey, it's great that I got to meet you today! I won't feel so lost and alone when I walk into my new homeroom."

"Don't worry about it. It's not that bad." Ricki nodded to the new classmate. "And if you ever feel like breathing some stable air, in spite of Rondo, you're always welcome at our place or at Mercy Ranch. Carlotta's always glad to have some people around to help out."

Beth looked a little bewildered. "Mercy Ranch?"

Lillian pointed over her shoulder. "Back there, where we just came from, that's Mercy Ranch. It's a shelter for ill and aging rescue horses, and the lady who started it is Carlotta Mancini, a former circus rider. She's really great, and always ready to listen to us if we have any problems."

Cathy nodded. "She sure is! By the way, this is Rashid. He belongs to Carlotta, but she lent him to me to ride and take care of. Terrific, huh?" Caught up in her enthusiasm, Cathy hadn't thought about how Beth must feel right now as far as horses went.

The girl swallowed and forced herself to smile pleasantly.

"That's... that's great! She must really be nice, this Carlotta. Well, I'll see you; I have to get back home, too. My mom's probably starting to wonder if I've run away, I've been gone so long."

"Okay, see you Monday. We'll meet by the bike rack in front of the school, okay?"

"Great! Thanks! I'm glad I ran into you guys. Bye!" Beth jumped on her bike and pedaled wildly.

"So long!" called Ricki after her.

"She's really okay, I think. What do you guys think?" asked Cathy, watching her ride away on her bike.

"I think so, too."

"At any rate, she's as crazy about horses as we are."

"You think so?"

"Of course," said Kevin. "I can tell."

"The thing with Rondo is going to depress her for awhile."

"True, but I bet she'll feel comfortable in a stable again quickly. There's bound to be a horse at Carlotta's that will help her get over Rondo's loss."

"Hey, did she ever tell us her name?" asked Lillian suddenly.

"No. She'll have to remain a nameless woman of mystery until Monday," Kevin wisecracked.

"Oh, Kev, I guess I'm going to have to keep my eyes on you," laughed Ricki and pinched her boyfriend in the ribs. "I happen to know that you love secrets, and as far as girls go –"

"Hmmm... now you're giving me ideas," said Kevin, winking.

"You guys can flirt at home! We're late already! Let's get going," warned Lillian, and she urged her white horse onward.

"Actually, I wish we could ride for another hour," reflected Cathy. "I still have to do my math homework."

"Oh, you poor thing! Thankfully, I'm already done with that," Ricki responded, taking a deep breath. She urged Diablo into a short trot to catch up to Holli. "But, you know what, as much as I love riding, I'll be glad when we get home. I'm starving!"

Kevin groaned. "Don't remind me about dinner. I'm still full of pie."

* * *

Warren Pendleton and his daughter arrived home about the same time and ran into each other in front of the garage of the new house.

Annoyed, the man made a face.

"Where have you been, Beth? I thought you'd be

48

helping your mother put things away. Instead, you're out hike riding on the very first day here!"

"I *did* help her, unlike you!" answered Beth defiantly.

"Excuse me? Did I just hear you correctly? Perhaps my dear daughter has noticed that I have a job? A job that finances all of her little pleasures and comforts."

"Yeah, yeah, whatever. Leave me alone!" she grumbled to herself. Ever since he had sold Rondo without asking her permission or telling her beforehand, she was really fed up with him.

"What did you just say? Now, you listen to me – I work all day, sometimes into the night, in order to provide my family with a good life. I talk myself crazy with potential customers, who end up backing out of deals... You have no idea what work is!"

Beth pretended to smile. "Okay, I'm sorry," she said, but it was obvious from the look on her face that she didn't mean it.

"Hmm..."

The girl quickly ran past her father and into the house in order to avoid any further discussion. Now all she needed was an excuse to get out of eating dinner with her parents. She was so furious with her father that she didn't want to sit down at the table with him. She was tired of hearing the word *work* from him, and as far as Rondo was concerned –

"He doesn't even realize that he's ruining everything!" she said to herself softly, and went up to her room as quietly as possible.

* * *

When it got dark, Carlotta went to the stable to check on everything, as she did every evening. She had gotten into the habit of doing that before she sat down in front of the television and made herself comfortable for at least another hour before going to bed.

Today, however, she spent more time with the horses than usual, and this time, after giving a few affectionate words to each one, she sat down on the little bench in the corridor that she had put there a few days earlier.

Lost in thought, she looked from one stall to another. How satisfied the animals seemed, munching their hay! It had been quite a while since any of them had shown signs of discontent or mistrust. They sensed that nothing bad would come from Carlotta or the kids who came and went each day. It seemed almost as though the badly mistreated horses had forgotten their former painful lives over the last few months.

Carlotta sighed deeply.

That Pendleton man, and the other men on the building board, probably couldn't believe that she'd rejected their offer. She lived her life for these poor horses and she would do everything in her power to see that they would be able to live out their lives without fear on Mercy Ranch.

"People don't tear down nursing homes to build hotels either," she mumbled quietly to herself.

Old Jonah, whom Carlotta had saved from being put down, pricked up his ears at her words and rumbled in a low whinny. It sounded almost like a confirmation to the former circus performer.

She nodded to the old boy and smiled.

"See, Jonah, that's the way it is. The world can be a cruel place sometimes. People still think there's a huge difference between man and animals, and it seems as though your lives, in comparison to the lives of humans, aren't worth anything. I will never understand how people can think that way."

Jonah listened attentively, but when Carlotta stopped talking he turned to the rest of his hay in the rack. To Jonah, as long as he had enough to eat, the humans could do whatever they wanted.

Pensively, Carlotta stretched out her legs, crossed her arms in front of her and then leaned back against the stable wall.

Suddenly she nodded yes.

She had decided then and there to submit the building plans for the little riding hall, which had lain in her drawer for four weeks. She'd go to the town hall on Monday. That would be her way of showing that she didn't intend to change her mind regarding Mr. Pendleton's offer.

Fortunately, she had talked with Otis Gates several months ago about her plans, and he had assured her that it was not a problem for her to construct a small riding hall on her property and that the approval of the community building board was just a formality.

Relieved at the thought of her new plan, Carlotta was

in a good mood as she got up a little stiffly, turned out the light in the stable, and went through the door at the end of the corridor into her house.

Monday morning she would pay Mayor Gates a visit, without calling in advance, and lay her plans before him. The woman tried to stifle a yawn.

I don't think I need any television tonight to help me fall asleep, she said to herself after glancing at the clock. It was later than she thought, so she went straight into the bathroom. Shortly thereafter, she took a shower, so she didn't hear the persistent ringing of the telephone. Whoever it was would have to wait till tomorrow in order to speak with Carlotta.

* * *

Beth had slept long and well the first night in her new room. As she stretched and yawned, blinking in the first rays of sunshine that had tickled her awake, she realized that she felt much better about living here today. Just yesterday she had met some really nice kids, and the probability that there were several stables nearby where she could hang out when she felt the need to be near horses, gave her a good feeling.

Horses...

She was instantly wide awake, trying as hard as she could to remember her dream. What was it again? What had her mother said to her last night?

"Dream something wonderful! You know, your first dream in your new home will come true."

Oh, if only she could remember. The one thing that she recalled right now was that she had galloped across a wide meadow on Rondo, and then they had ridden through some small woods before resting near one of the most beautiful lakes that Beth had ever seen.

Sighing, the girl sat up.

She'd have no luck with that dream, she decided. She would never be able to ride Rondo again. She would never feel his soft breath in her hair as she brushed his velvety coat dry after a wonderful ride. She would never again hear his low whinny when he greeted her, and never again see the shine in his eyes that showed how glad he was to see her standing in front of his stall.

Suddenly, the good feeling that Beth had when she awakened was gone. Would her longing for Rondo ever stop? Would she ever be able to accept that she would never see him again?

The girl bit her lips to stop herself from crying again, as she had so often in the last few days when she thought of her horse. She wondered how he was at that moment. She wondered if his new owner would take good care of him.

Maybe he's already forgotten me, she thought as she slowly got dressed. But she didn't really believe that.

Chapter 4

As they did every afternoon, the kids got together at Ricki's. Now they were sitting in her room while she looked for the photos of Golden Star that Gwen had sent her.

"Too bad we didn't ask that nice new girl we met where she lives. We could have hung out with her this afternoon, welcomed her to the town.... Darn it, where did I put those photos?" Ricki rummaged through her desk drawer.

Kevin watched his girlfriend and laughed. "It's official, your desk is messier than mine."

"Do you think you'll find those photos any time today?" teased Lillian.

"People who are too tidy are just too lazy to look for things," Ricki admonished them, "Don't worry. I can find my way around my own chaos," she said, pulling a large manila envelope from the depths of her desk drawer and waving it in the air. "Here they are!"

"Oh, terrific! Let's have a look."

"Wow... that's Golden Star?"

"His coat is a little darker, isn't it?"

"But he looks fabulous! I'd really love to see him again. Do you guys think he would still know us?" asked Cathy, her eyes shining.

"I bet not. After all, it was a long time ago; remember, when we were there he had just been born."

"Are we going riding this afternoon?" Ricki asked.

Lillian groaned loudly. "Look out the window. Have you seen the condition of the horses? Holli's no longer white, he's so covered with mud. I can guarantee you that I won't get that off today. And your four-legged friends don't look any better."

"To be honest, I don't really feel like getting into a messy grooming marathon just now," admitted Cathy.

"Then why don't we just let our horses have a whole day to exercise by themselves on the paddock?" Ricki suggested. "But if we're not going riding, what are we going to do with the rest of the day?"

"Why don't we *saddle* our bikes and go downtown? The ice-cream parlor reopened a couple of days ago." Kevin was always thinking of his stomach.

"Oh, ice cream! Great idea!"

"Then let's go. I'm beginning to forget what it tastes like. The winter was just too long."

Laughing, the kids got up and left the house. A short time later they were riding their bikes along the road that led into town.

Diablo and his stable mates stood lazily on the paddock and dozed in the shadow of the huge pear tree.

The horses' tails constantly swished away the insects that buzzed around them. Diablo kept kicking his hind legs against his belly when suddenly a wasp, attracted by his hot, sweaty coat, stung him on the croup. Diablo separated from the others and trotted a few feet around the tree in order to try to outrun the painful itching.

He went down on his knees right next to the tree trunk. Instinct told him that he would find relief by rolling around in the wet grass. The motion he made as he rolled back and forth brought him nearer and nearer to the tree trunk, which blocked his efforts to pull himself to a standing position.

Holli and Rashid looked over at their friend, but the others didn't even notice his unfortunate situation.

Diablo tried again and again to get up; unable to do so, he kicked violently and struck the tree trunk with his left hind hoof, scraping his leg on the hard bark and lacerating his coat and the thin skin over the tendons.

The black horse tried several more times to get up, but each time he only made his position worse. Finally he gave up, exhausted, and just lay there, in pain and confusion, patiently waiting for someone to find him and free him from this awful predicament.

* * *

No one could accuse Cass of not making an honest effort to trust Rondo. For the first two weeks after her parents gave her the gray Arabian, she was able to force herself to go to the riding stable every day and get to know and feel at ease around the gentle animal. However, the fear that Ashanti had instilled in her was so deeply rooted that she interpreted even the slightest motion from Rondo, like when he pricked up his ears, as a sign that he was about to attack her, and she fled from his stall in a panic.

"Come on, Cass," Chad Cameron, who had been observing the girl during that two-week getting-acquainted period, said. "I have only three riders in my class today. This would be a good time for you to join in and ride with us on Rondo."

Deep inside, Cass knew that she could only overcome her fear if she managed to ride her new horse, presuming of course, that the ride went smoothly, without any problems. So she obeyed the riding instructor without saying a word and saddled her horse with trembling hands.

As she led him into the ring, the image of Ashanti lying on the floor came back to her. *What if Rondo were to act like that? What if he fell and –?*

"I know what you're thinking right now, Cass," Cameron said softly, as he approached her and took hold of Rondo's reins. "It's never easy to overcome your fears and try again. That's just the way it is in life... in *all* aspects of life."

"You may not see it this way, but your father has given you a great gift in Rondo: a second chance to face up to and overcome the fear – phobia, really – that prevents you from participating in one of the most thrilling athletic experiences a young person can have. The thing is, though, you have to want it!" He paused. "But enough sermonizing from me. Rondo is a very reliable horse. You've watched Beth ride him many times during class, and you've seen what a gentle animal he is. So trust him, and he'll trust you."

Cass nodded silently. *Oh, only if it were that simple.* Nervously, she fumbled with the girth.

"Slow down, take a deep breath, and be deliberate, confident with your movements." Cameron urged calmly. "As you know, horses are very sensitive to their riders' moods, so if Rondo senses your insecurity, it can transfer to him. If you stay cool, he will too."

"Yeah, yeah," Cass mumbled as she offered up a silent prayer to heaven before mounting.

Chad Cameron smiled. "There, see. You've made a start. Ride around the ring a few times with loose reins at a walking pace so you two can get to know each other. You'll see, at the end of the lesson you won't want to dismount." He smiled at her encouragingly before taking a step back. "Okay, get going."

Cass nodded and then, her heart thumping, she gave Rondo the sign to walk. After leading the gelding along the side rail for several turns around the ring, she shortened the reins and dared to let the horse begin to trot.

Cameron nodded approvingly. "All right," he murmured. "Good job." He turned around to check on the other riders, who were exercising their horses before the riding lesson began. And then it happened.

Ted Hinds, another of Cameron's students who wanted to participate in the riding lesson on his Orlando, was late. From outside the stable he shouted, "Is the door clear?!" and, without waiting for an answer, swung it open, causing a near collision with Cass, who was just passing that spot on Rondo.

Startled, the horse took a mighty step sideways. The girl screamed and tensed up in the saddle. She pulled on the reins, taking Rondo completely out of his rhythm and causing him to bump into a nearby horse. What followed was mayhem: a multi-horse, chain-reaction pileup of kicking, panicky animals, their young riders struggling in vain to get them under control. When Rondo turned suddenly on his hind legs to avoid the crush, Cass lost her balance and fell to the ground.

"Hinds!" Chad yelled at the young boy, who was staring, transfixed, at the chaos he had created in the riding hall. "You know you can't just tear open the stable door like that without some kind of warning. Look what you've done to Cass," he said, running over to the fallen young girl, who was pressing her hand against her ankle, her face distorted with pain.

"Come on, you have to get those boots off," the riding instructor said, and he led the limping girl out into the hallway, where Amber, another rider, had hitched Rondo to the railing.

Cass sat down on the bench and screamed as Cameron pulled off the boot.

"Nothing's broken," he determined with a sigh of relief, and asked Amber to take Rondo back to his stall.

"Your ankle's a little bruised, but it's not serious," he told Cass. "In a few days, you can get back in the saddle."

The girl looked at him, her eyes enormous, and she began to shake her head slowly. "I am never going to ride again, Mr. Cameron! Maybe I shouldn't have taken up riding. Every time I ride, something bad happens, so before I cause another animal or human to get hurt, I'm going to stop."

"That's nonsense." Cameron tried to object, but Cass gestured for him to stop.

"You have no idea. I started riding only because all of my friends did, but I've always been afraid to be around horses. It got worse with Ashanti, and even... even with Rondo, I'm more afraid than anyone can imagine." She looked at her riding instructor sadly. "It doesn't have anything to do with Rondo – he's gentle enough – I just don't want anything to do with horses – ever! I just hope my parents will understand," she added, whispering, tears in her eyes. Cameron sensed that he had completely lost his student after all.

Slowly, he nodded. "Okay, Cass," he said, his voice thick. "I understand, although I really think it's too bad. You're right, though. Being afraid of horses is the worst possible predisposition a rider can have. I'll call your mother and ask her to come and pick you up. You can't walk home on that injured ankle."

"Thank you." Cass turned away and took one last look

at Rondo, who was watching her from his stall with his gentle eyes.

"I'm so sorry, Rondo. Please forgive me," she whispered with a lump in her throat as she got up. She took her grooming kit in one hand and her boot in the other, and then limped down the corridor toward the stable door, so that she could wait for her mother in front of the riding hall.

It was the last time in her life Cass would ever enter a riding stable.

* * *

After trying to reach Carlotta by phone unsuccessfully, Warren J. Pendleton decided to meet with the farmers with whom he had spoken individually the previous day. He knew his offer was tempting, and he was confident he'd be able to do business with the farmers.

"I can't say when I'll be home tonight," he called to his wife, before getting into the car and driving off. "Got to see some local farmers," he offered by way of explanation.

Nancy Pendleton watched him leave through the window and sighed deeply. For quite a while now conversations between the couple had been stiff, formal, limited to just what was necessary, and lacking in affection. While Nancy suffered greatly from this, it didn't seem to bother Warren at all that their marriage seemed to be falling apart.

She was so glad that at least she had Beth.

"How did you sleep in your new surroundings?" she asked her daughter, who appeared in the kitchen only after her father had driven off.

"Pretty well, thanks."

"Would you help me later with a few small things? I want to move some of the furniture around, and the pieces are too heavy for me to lift by myself. Also, I found a few boxes that probably belong to you. Maybe you could unpack them this morning."

"Yeah, of course. No problem." Beth reached for a piece of toast and spread it thickly with jam.

"By the way, I met a few of my new classmates yesterday when I was out on my bike exploring our new town. They seemed really nice. They ride..."

"Oh, that's terrific! I'm really glad!" Nancy responded, but Beth could tell that her mother's enthusiasm was forced, and that her thoughts were elsewhere.

The girl interrupted her chewing and said abruptly, "Why don't you get a divorce? He's just plain obnoxious!"

Shocked, Nancy looked up. "You shouldn't talk like that about your father, Beth."

"Why not? It's plain to see that you two don't get along anymore. He... he's changed a lot over the last few years."

"That's true, but nevertheless, I want to ask you to –"

"Oh, come on, Mom, I'm not a child."

"But you're not old enough to understand all of the reasons..."

"But –"

"I don't want to talk about it anymore!" her mother cut her off.

"There's a horse stable near here. I'd like to go there at noon," the girl said, trying to change the subject.

"Okay, go ahead. Do they sell bread there?"

"What?" Confused, Beth looked at her mother; then she realized how distracted her mother was. "Oh, sorry... I know what you want. Well, there's a bakery two streets away, and the supermarket is about ten minutes from here."

Nancy smiled. "That sounds good. Then we'll have fresh rolls for dinner again, starting tomorrow," she promised as she began to clear away the breakfast dishes.

* * *

It was early afternoon before Beth finally got on her bike. She had helped her mother diligently, and now she planned to ride around for a few hours and see what there was to see in this town with a clear conscience.

She pedaled slowly through the tree-lined streets, taking in the details of her new hometown.

This little town is bigger than I thought, she realized to her surprise and then she came to an abrupt stop, startled by the loud voices calling behind her.

"Heeey!"

"Helloooo!"

"Stop!"

When she turned around, she recognized the kids she had seen the day before on horseback. They were laughing and waving to her from a table outside the ice-cream shop.

Beth's expression relaxed and she rode across the street to her new classmates. "Sorry, I didn't see you as I rode past."

"Come join us." Ricki pointed to a vacant chair at their table. "The ice cream here is terrific!"

"Really? If I'd known I'd have brought some money with me," Beth replied, looking a little disappointed. "I was actually planning on going somewhere else."

Lillian opened her wallet and looked inside: "You're in luck! Just enough for a strawberry sundae, if you want."

"Thanks, but that's not necessary," objected Beth.

"Of course it's not 'necessary.' I said, 'if you want.'"

"Of course 'I want'! Thanks, next time it'll be on me."

"You'll have plenty of opportunities to do that," grinned Kevin. "Where were you headed? Maybe we can tell you the quickest way to get there."

"I wanted to go to that Mercy Ranch you showed me yesterday."

"Lucky again!" Lillian, who had just ordered Beth's sundae, nodded to her. "We've decided to go see Carlotta, too."

"That's great!" Beth had gotten her ice cream and, between spoonfuls, she studied her new friends. She was grateful to be in the company of such nice kids. She was beginning to feel at home, less like an outsider.

"This is totally awesome," she said, and rolled her eyes in enjoyment. "Looks like I'll be leaving my allowance here on a regular basis."

"Why should you be any different from us? In the summer, we're always broke."

"I can imagine."

"Hey, are you dreading tomorrow, I mean school?" Ricki asked.

Beth shook her head. "Not really. Not since I met you guys," she beamed at Ricki.

"Thanks!"

After a while, when Beth finished her ice cream, the kids got up and got back on their bikes.

"Come on, let's take a little detour," Ricki suggested. "We'll ride by Echo Lake. You just have to get to know it. Hey, by the way, what's your name?"

Beth turned bright red. She had actually forgotten to tell them her name.

"It's Elizabeth, but everybody calls me Beth. What's yours?"

"Well, Beth, I'm Ricki. The others are Lillian, Cathy, and Kevin."

"Pleased to meet you all!"

As the kids pedaled their way toward Echo Lake, Lillian, who was riding next to their new acquaintance, gave in to her growing curiosity.

"So, Beth, why don't you tell us a little about yourself?"

"There's not much to tell, really. I'm fourteen, I have no siblings, and I used to have a horse, but you know that already."

"What kind of horse was it?"

"An Arabian, but I don't want to talk about that right now."

I just sounded like Mom, realized Beth, after the words had left her lips.

"It's okay. We have to turn left here, by the way." Cathy pointed across the intersection and, after the kids had all turned left, Beth suddenly felt as though her heart had skipped a beat.

That's impossible! she thought, and she had to catch her breath. *It can't be! It's impossible!* She breathed deeply and tried to suppress her memory, but after a few minutes, when they reached the banks of Echo Lake, a small cry burst out of her. She almost rode into a big rock that she hadn't seen as she got a look at the water.

"Hey, what's with you?" shouted Kevin in surprise.

"The path through the woods... the lake..." Beth stammered and swallowed excitedly.

"Yeah, and? What about it?"

"I... last night I rode down *this* path to *this* lake..."

"What?"

"What do you mean by that?"

Beth couldn't find the words to explain what she meant. Much later, when she had calmed down, she asked the others, "Do you guys think that some dreams do come true? I mean, last night I had a dream about this place I've only just now seen for the first time."

Ricki looked at her from the side, and smiled knowingly.

"Of course! It happens to me a lot."

"Honestly?"

"Yeah."

Beth closed her eyes for a moment.

"If that's true, then... then I'm going to see Rondo again!"

* * *

Carlotta was reviewing the applications for her youth summer program at the ranch when she looked through the window and saw Ricki and her friends arriving. A few minutes later someone knocked on her office door.

"Carlotta, are you there?" Cathy shouted from the hallway.

"Where else would I be?" the owner of Mercy Ranch laughed, and pushed the papers aside. The girl peered in from the doorway.

"We brought someone with us. I hope that's okay with you."

"As long as it's not a tax collector or the sheriff, I don't see a problem. Go on into the kitchen. I'll be right there."

"Great!" Cathy disappeared.

Well, let's see who Ricki's brought with her this time, Carlotta thought to herself as she picked up her cane and limped her way to the kitchen.

"Carlotta, this is Beth," Ricki introduced the new girl to Carlotta. "She's just moved to town and is going to be in our class starting tomorrow. She likes horses and she can ride."

"Hello, Mrs. Mancini, I've heard a lot about you," Beth greeted her pleasantly.

"I hope only good things," replied Carlotta heartily. "If you like horses, then you're at the right place here at Mercy Ranch. There are a few veteran horses that are always looking for loving hands and gentle words. How long have you been in the area? And how long have you been riding?"

"We – my mother and father and I – arrived in town just yesterday. I've been riding for about five years." Beth's expression became distant. "I had my own horse until recently –"

"Which her father sold without even telling her! Isn't that outrageous?" Cathy completed the girl's story.

Carlotta looked straight at Beth. "Is that true?"

The girl nodded sadly.

"But why?"

"I have no idea! I guess it seemed easier to him to buy me a new horse when we got settled here than to organize a transport of the 'old one'."

"So he wants to buy you a new horse?"

"At least that's what he said, but I doubt he'll really do it. Anyway, I don't want a new horse. I want my Rondo back." Beth's looked off into the distance, and Carlotta could sense the girl's longing for her four-legged friend.

"And what if you tried to talk to your father again?"

Beth snorted contemptuously. "You can't talk with my father! He's a monster!"

"Now, now, he can't be that bad, can he?"

"No, actually he's even worse!"

"Carlotta, couldn't you talk to him?" Kevin dared to ask.

"Young man, I don't even know Beth's father, and who knows what his reasons were for selling the horse."

"Does that mean that you approve of him just selling the horse without even telling Beth?" Lillian demanded to know.

Carlotta frowned angrily. "Of course I don't approve of such a sale, but I'm not going to make judgments about a person I don't know anything about."

"But –"

"Oh, please," Beth interrupted. "I don't want you to fight because of me! It won't bring Rondo back, and it won't make my father any easier to like." Beth smiled apologetically at Carlotta. "May I see your horses?"

"Of course! Maybe there'll be one that appeals to you, that you'd like to spend a little time with." Carlotta put her hand encouragingly on Beth's shoulder.

"Yes, maybe," Beth answered softly.

Chapter 5

"Thank goodness that's finished!" Jake, the groom at the Sulais' stable, gave one last look around the stable before grabbing the broom and putting it away in the tack room. A glance at the clock told him that the horses could stay on the paddock for at least another hour and a half before being brought back in and put in their stalls.

By that time the kids will probably be here, the old man thought and headed back to his cottage to have some dinner.

Stepping outside the stable, he looked over at the paddock, as he always did. The sight of "his horses" never failed to fill his old heart with joy and satisfaction, but today, even with his failing eyesight, Jake could see that something wasn't quite right. One of his four-legged charges was lying stretched straight out under a tree, and the others were scattered all over the paddock, moving slowly forward and grazing.

It wasn't that unusual for horses to lie down in the meadow during the day, but Jake's gut feeling, on which he could usually rely, told him that something must have happened that was out of the ordinary.

As fast as he could, he started off toward the paddock. When he saw that it was his favorite, Diablo, who was lying motionless in the grass, his already weak heart beat so fast that he nearly fainted.

"Oh, no, what's happened?" Jake whispered. "Diablo!" he called with a trembling voice as he crawled through the paddock fence and ran over to the horse. "What's wrong, Diablo? Get up!"

At the sound of the familiar voice, Diablo turned his head toward Jake, who knelt down beside the horse and stroked his neck comfortingly with shaking hands.

After assessing the situation, it was clear to Jake that Diablo would be able to stand up if he were turned over on his other side. However, it was also clear to the elderly groom that he would not be able to do this alone. It would take at least two people to roll the heavy animal over on his back.

Jake's mind raced feverishly. Ricki's parents and her kid brother, Harry, were at a soccer game, and the kids were... somewhere. Desperate, he looked at Diablo, who just lay there calmly.

"Don't be afraid, my boy, we're going to get you back up on your legs, somehow," Jake said softly and got up. He hated to leave the horse alone, but he had no choice.

He needed help. He'd go to his cottage and try phoning everyone he could think of.

Back at his cottage, he opened an old, worn address book that lay beside the telephone and leafed through the pages until he came to Ricki's cell phone number.

"Oh, Ricki, I'm glad I reached you," he began hastily, before he realized that the voice he heard was just her voice mail. He hated talking to those things. "Darn it!" Frustrated, he was going to hang up, but then he changed his mind. This was too important. He'd leave a message:

"This is Jake," he said, trying to keep the panic out of his voice. "Diablo has taken a fall and is lying on his side in the paddock. He can't get up by himself, and I can't turn him over without help. Wherever you are, come home immediately. I need you... Diablo needs you."

Then he thought about Carlotta. Of course, Carlotta would know what to do. He dialed her number. She was sure to come right away to help him, and there was a good chance Ricki and her friends were at Mercy Ranch.

"Pick up, Carlotta!"

* * *

Beth had spent two wonderful hours with her new friends at Mercy Ranch. *They were right about Carlotta*, she said to herself after she'd met the woman. *She's terrific. She made me feel right at home*. And it had been great to be around horses again. But being so close to so many sweet, affectionate animals made her miss her Rondo even more. When she couldn't bear it any longer, she said a quick good bye, got on her bike, and pedaled home, trying to leave the memory of her horse behind her.

* * *

"Hey, Carlotta, any chance the riding hall construction will begin this year?" Lillian asked. "We're all looking forward to riding in comfort next winter."

"Who knows?" Carlotta shrugged her shoulders. "I had hoped that it would be ready by winter, but it all depends on how quickly the mayor goes over my plans and submits my proposal to the town council. This kind of permit can get tied up for weeks sometimes."

"What? That long? It's such a good idea, I'd have thought it would be approved quickly." Lillian made a disappointed grimace.

"Me too, but with that land developer showing up from out of nowhere, and starting to buy up property, it could ruin my plans. It's all about money. You see, the city will consider what would bring in more revenue: a small private riding hall or a public golf course. And at the end of the day, I could be refused a permit."

"Would that mean you'd have to sell the ranch?" Kevin wanted to know.

Carlotta shook her head firmly. "No, my boy! That's the one thing I can promise you all. Mercy Ranch, and all that goes with it, will never be replaced by a golf course. The worst that can happen is that there won't be a riding hall, but my old guests aren't about to lose their homes, ever again."

Carlotta tapped her cane on Kevin's handlebars. "So,

my dears, that's it for today. I think it's time for you to go home. I still have some paperwork to finish."

"Okay, I imagine Jake wouldn't mind us getting home on time for once, so that we can help him bring the horses in from the paddock." Ricki grabbed her bike and got on.

"And I'll probably spend a few hours today turning my muddy jumper back into a white horse," groaned Lillian.

Carlotta laughed.

"Then you still have a lot to do today. Well, take care and say hello to your new friend for me tomorrow. I wish her a good start at school. Oh, and tell her that if she wants to, she can come here any time. I think she has a way with Silver and I bet he wouldn't object at all to some regular exercise."

Cathy beamed. "You mean Beth can ride Silver whenever she wants? She's going to be happy about that!"

Carlotta gestured vaguely. "I'm not so sure she'll be that happy. After all, her heart and thoughts are still with Rondo, and I can understand that. But maybe Silver can help her get over the loss of her horse more quickly. It's at least worth a try."

"I agree!" commented Ricki. "But you have to admit, it was really mean of her father just to sell the horse without telling her."

Carlotta objected. "We've already discussed that topic, and since I don't know the details I'll say no more. But perhaps you should remember that at least the horse was sold to another rider and not to some farmer who might

74

work him to death! That means he's probably doing better than we think. The new owner is probably enjoying Rondo, and we should just let the whole thing rest. Don't you agree?"

Ricki made a face. "I don't know. Of course it could be just as you say, but what if it isn't, and Rondo –"

"Ricki!" Carlotta cut her off.

The girl sighed. "Okay, Carlotta, I know. We're not supposed to imagine the worst every time."

"Exactly. Now, get going. I don't feel like staying up all night doing my paperwork. After all, I'm an old woman and I need my sleep."

"See you!" Kevin called out over his shoulder, as the kids started off toward home on their bikes.

"And yet," Ricki said pensively, "I have the feeling that the topic of Rondo isn't closed – for anybody."

* * *

When Beth got home she found her mother standing in front of the washing machine, her eyes red from crying. She was furiously throwing one piece of clothing after another into the round opening.

"Mom... Mom? Did something happen?"

Nancy Pendleton shook her head wildly no.

"Are you sure?"

"Yes!"

"Hmmm, then why are you throwing the clothes –?"

"Your dinner's on the kitchen table," Beth's mother said brusquely. "I made grilled ham and cheese sandwiches."

"Oh, great, my favorite," Beth said as she quickly disappeared into the kitchen. She was hungry, and the sandwiches looked good, but her mother's mood had ruined her appetite. As long as she didn't know why her mother was crying, Beth couldn't eat anything.

She was about to wrap the sandwiches in plastic wrap and put them in the refrigerator when Nancy, an apologetic smile on her face, entered the kitchen.

"I'm sorry I snapped at you, sweetie. I didn't even say hello. How was your afternoon? Did you enjoy yourself? You'll be back in school tomorrow and won't have much free time."

"I had a great afternoon, Mom. I ran into those kids I met yesterday. They bought me ice cream and then we rode our bikes to a place called Mercy Ranch. The owner, a middle-aged lady named Carlotta, is really cool. She opened the ranch a few years ago as a shelter for rescue horses."

"That's really nice! I think it's great you've been able to make new friends so quickly. And there's a horse farm near here? Well, then, I'll know where to look for you from now on."

Beth shrugged her shoulders. "I'm not sure whether or not I'll go back."

"Why not? I thought you said you liked it there." Confused, Nancy gazed at her daughter.

"Yeah, I do. Absolutely! But when I'm around horses I keep thinking about Rondo, and it makes me almost crazy to realize that I'll never see him again."

"Time heals all wounds, Beth. I'm sure you'll never forget him, but the memory will fade and, one day, it will begin to be fun to be around horses again," said Nancy, trying to comfort her, but Beth disagreed.

"The memory of my Rondo will never fade! Did you know that Dad was planning on selling him?"

"No, I knew nothing about it! Has your father ever talked to me about anything relating to business?"

"I have no idea! Does he talk to you at all? All I hear is, 'I'm leaving, and I don't know when I'll be home.'"

Beth saw her mother make a fist and suddenly she understood.

"You were crying because of *him* again, weren't you?"

Her mother's silence confirmed her suspicions. "I should have known. He pleases himself and doesn't even notice how unhappy you are!"

"He works hard to provide a nice life for us!" Nancy offered her standard defense of her husband. She had so hoped that here, in this new place, they could make a fresh start, and that Warren would spend more time with her and Beth. However, it was easy to see, even in the first few days, that his business interests were much more important to him than his family.

Beth snorted contemptuously. "Work! That's all that interests him. What do you have to do, become one of his clients before he'll spend any time with you? It seems he always has enough time for *them*." She looked at her mother sadly. "Maybe you should just go away for a few days, Mom," she said slowly and softly. "Give him a chance to find out if he really cares about you... what it's like to be without you."

Nancy stared at her daughter. *Wise child,* she thought to herself. *Why didn't I think of that? Someone's got to do something to let Warren know he's in danger of losing his family. It's up to me.*

Yes, she was going to give it a try. Even if it was just for three or four days, she was going to leave Warren on his own. It would be enough time to make him think about what his family means to him.

"What would you say to not starting school until *next* Monday?" she asked, out of the blue.

"Huh? What do you mean?" It had been her mother who had urged her to go back to school as soon as possible so that she wouldn't miss too much because of the move.

"I could say that our move was delayed..."

Beth opened her eyes wider. "Mom, have you, uhhh..."

"No, I have not lost my mind!" she answered her daughter's unspoken question. "What would you think about visiting Rondo?"

Beth turned white. "I... of course... but..." she stammered incoherently.

"Then throw three T-shirts, a sweatshirt, some underwear and a raincoat into your backpack and hurry up. I want to leave before your father gets home."

Beth shot out of the room. A thousand thoughts went through her head as she tore open her closet door and started stuffing her clothes into an overnight bag. She couldn't believe her mother was acting so impulsively on a suggestion that Beth had just thrown out.

"Whatever!" she said out loud. She was going to see Rondo, and that was the most important thing to her right now.

* * *

Jake waited anxiously for Carlotta to arrive. She had agreed to come immediately. The kids were already heading home on their bikes, so she couldn't tell them about Jake's call.

"If I catch up to them, we'll stow Ricki's bike in the trunk and I'll take her with me. If not, then somehow you and I will find a way to free Diablo from his terrible situation." Carlotta hadn't waited for an answer, but just put down the receiver immediately, got in her car, and drove off as fast as she could.

Halfway there she caught up with the kids and, telling Ricki there was a problem at home, asked her to get in. She didn't tell her the whole story about what had happened until they were on their way again, and now the girl was sitting, pale and quiet, in the passenger seat.

"It's not that bad, Ricki," Carlotta said, trying to calm the girl. "Things like this happen every once in a while."

"How long has he been lying there? When we rode off he was standing under the tree with all the others."

"I don't know. Jake didn't give me any details." Carlotta concentrated on the road and a good ten minutes later the car slid a little and came to a stop on the field path in front of the paddock.

Jake was standing near Diablo and waving at them with impatience. "Good thing you're here. He's getting restless!" he yelled.

Ricki knelt down at her horse's head. "What did you do?" she asked softly, and swallowed hard with concern. Then her glance fell on the two rope lines that were lying in the grass next to Jake. "What are those for?"

"You'll see in a minute." The groom reached for one of the lines and bent over Diablo's legs.

"Okay, my boy, hold still. If you do we'll be finished quicker!" he whispered to the horse as he wrapped the middle of the line loosely around the ankle of the back leg that was lying on the ground. Then he gave the ends to Ricki and told her to hold them taut behind Diablo's back, so that they wouldn't slide off his ankle. He repeated this with the front leg that was lying on the ground and then placed himself in the same position as Ricki while Carlotta snapped a long rope to Diablo's halter.

"On the count of three, we all pull together. We should try to roll our boy over on his back and onto his other side on the first attempt. When the tree is no longer in the way, he'll be able to stand up easily. Ricki, as soon as Diablo is lying correctly, let go of the line so that it loosens up on his ankle. Carlotta, don't let him go until we get the lines off his legs."

"Aye, aye, Captain. Here we go. One... two... threeeeee!"

Ricki and Jake pulled with all their might on the ends of the lines, and it looked as if they were not going to be able to move the heavy giant onto his other side, but when Diablo sensed that his legs were free and up in the air, he gave an enormous jerk. Using his own strength, he catapulted himself almost into the right position and then jumped up immediately.

"Let go!" shouted Jake to Ricki, but he didn't need to. Her line was already lying on the ground. She had quickly jumped over to Diablo's head so that she could calm him. Carlotta still held tightly to the rope attached to his halter.

Carefully, Jake untied the horse's legs, and then allowed himself to breathe a sigh of relief.

"Phew! We did it! I never would have managed that by myself!"

"And you're sure that Diablo is really okay?" asked Ricki.

"He has a little brush burn on his left hind leg, but that's not serious. We'll spray it with antiseptic, and in a few days it'll be forgotten." Jake took a few steps backward. "Now let him go. He'll be relieved that he can move again."

Diablo tried to take a few steps and, since he didn't have any pain, he raced off to join his stable companions.

Ricki rolled up the two lines. "Boy, am I glad he's up again! Thank you both so much," she said, and gave Carlotta a hug and Jake a big kiss on his cheek. Her eyes were still glued on Diablo, who was now grazing peacefully.

"I'll be right there," she called after Jake, who had already started walking back to the stable. She said good-bye to Carlotta and then stood at the edge of the paddock as Lillian, Cathy, and Kevin rode up, panting and out of breath.

"Hey, is everything okay?" Cathy called from a distance.

Ricki laughed with obvious relief. "Yeah, everything's fine! Diablo got trapped on his side under the tree. We had two options ... either cut down the tree, or turn Diablo onto his other side!" It felt good to be able to joke again.

Kevin grinned.

"Since the tree's still there, I guess you guys must have worked hard," he commented.

"You can say that again. Diablo is definitely not a lightweight!"

* * *

Chad Cameron stood in front of Rondo's stall, deep in thought. "What are we going to do with you?" he asked softly as he observed the gray Arabian standing still, his head hanging.

Cass hadn't been to the stable since she fell off Rondo on her first attempt to ride him, and he hadn't seen her parents again either. He'd heard that they were trying to sell the horse, but hadn't yet found a buyer.

"If this goes on much longer, the problem will solve itself!" Noah Hickson, the stable groom, had said the day before. "This animal is depressed. He won't eat anything and he's losing weight daily. He misses having something to do, someone to pay attention to him. He misses Beth! Darn it, why did Mr. Pendleton have to sell this horse? That girl and Rondo were a real match. It's a shame they were separated."

Cameron sighed deeply. He didn't know who he felt more sorry for, but when he looked at the horse, he realized that Noah was right. It just couldn't go on like this. Sooner or later, the animal was going to die of loneliness.

"Don't give up, boy," he urged Rondo softly, before walking to the stable's small office. He wanted to look through the advertisements for the tournaments coming up in the next few weeks.

When Cameron left, Rondo lifted his head wearily and watched him go with listless eyes. He didn't understand the world any longer, or why no one was taking care of him.

The hay from that morning still lay untouched in his rack, and although the horse felt hungry, he just sniffed at it and turned away again. He gazed longingly along the corridor of the stable. His inner clock still worked, and it told him that it was about time for Beth to show up... but would she ever return?

Rondo missed his former owner terribly, and as long as no one else took care of him, he would never forget her.

So he stood for hours in his stall, motionless. Only when the light was turned off did he sink down onto the straw, disappointed and weary. Once again, the one for whom he had waited so long hadn't come.

* * *

After her friends left, Ricki sat alone in the stable on a bale of straw and watched Diablo as he munched his hay. She was so glad that he was okay after the mishap on the paddock. She longed for the day when school would be behind her. Life would have so much more purpose if she could spend all day with the horses. She envied Carlotta and her Mercy Ranch. It must be fabulous to lead a life like that. No school, no homework, no tests, no stress – well, at least no school stress, and work that involved horses wasn't really work, it was pure joy! Ricki closed her eyes for a moment to enjoy the thought.

"Hey!" Jake's gruff voice jolted her out of her reverie. "You're lucky I didn't lock you in here. I was just about to close up the stables when I heard you snoring!" Jake stood in front of her, teasing, his hands on his hips.

"Oh, Jake, you startled me!" Ricki said, walking over to Diablo's stall to say good night to her horse. As she wrapped her arms around his head, a shrill noise broke the quiet of the stalls. Startled, Diablo stepped back against the stall wall, and the other animals were disturbed as well.

Ricki took her cell phone out of her pants pocket and made an effort to stop the shrill ringing as quickly as possible.

Jake frowned. "Do you have to bring that thing into the stable? I've told you a hundred times that the horses need their peace and quiet! You can see how startled they were!"

"Sorry, Jake," Ricki said as she ran out of the stable, first to get away from Jake's lecture and second, so that she could talk on the phone in private.

"Okay, now I can hear you!" she said, holding the phone to her ear. "Who's there? Oh, Gwen! I'm so glad to hear your voice! How come you didn't call me on our home phone? Oh! What? No one's picking up? Where is everyone? I'll call you right back, okay? Bye."

84

Quickly, she ran into the house, grabbed the wireless phone, and shut herself in her room. A long conversation with her friend Gwen about horses, Golden Star, and the goings-on at Highland Farm Estates was just what she needed now. The fact that she had to study for a grammar test tomorrow completely slipped her mind.

Chapter 6

Carlotta brought the blueprints for her proposed riding ring to the town hall on Monday morning, but she didn't get to talk to Mayor Gates. When he learned that Mrs. Mancini was on her way, Gates instructed his secretary to tell Carlotta he wasn't in. He had no interest in further discussions with the woman. He would have to tell her that since she had turned down Mr. Pendleton's offer to purchase and develop her property, the mayor's office was no longer favorably inclined toward her plans for building a riding ring. Things were sure to get ugly.

"Well, tell him I'm sorry I missed him, and, if you would, ask him to look at these blueprints when he has a chance," Carlotta said with a friendly wink to the secretary, as she handed her the carefully prepared portfolio.

"Yes, of course, Mrs. Mancini, the minute he gets back."

In a good mood, Carlotta decided to drop by Brigitte

Sulai's house on her way home. Ricki's mother was a good friend, and she made a terrific cup of coffee.

* * *

"Hey, Carlotta, it's good to see you again so soon," Jake called to Carlotta as she got out of her car. "I didn't get to ask you yesterday – how's the ranch going? How are the animals? And how is it we usually see so little of you these days? Are you that busy?"

"Hi, Jake, I've missed you, too. The ranch is still standing, thanks, and the animals are enjoying their old age, and I have so much to do that sometimes I don't even know where to begin."

The groom grinned broadly. "Maybe you should hire someone full time to help you."

"I have enough help. You wouldn't believe how many teenagers are at the ranch all the time. There's never a day when there aren't at least five kids hanging out. For them there's nothing better than being around horses and cleaning out the stalls so that they can ride afterward. Oh, by the way, could you please tell Cathy when you see her this afternoon that the blacksmith is coming the beginning of next week. I don't know the exact time yet, but she should plan for either Monday or Tuesday afternoon."

Jake nodded. "Okay, I'll let her know."

Carlotta waved to him and was about to go over to the house when Jake took her by the arm and stopped her.

"Say, have you heard that there's a new real estate guy in town who's been calling all the farmers around here? Apparently he wants to buy a lot of property and meadowland, in order –"

"In order to build a hotel and a golf course," Carlotta finished Jake's sentence, sighing. "They've already asked me to sell my ranch, but that's not going to happen."

Jake laughed at first, but then he got serious. "You're going to have a tough time, Carlotta, and you're probably going to be the only one who refuses to sell."

"I don't care! After all, they can't force me, can they?"

"No, but believe me, this real estate guy is going to pull out all the stops to make your life on the ranch miserable if you end up ruining his plans."

"Oh, Jake, don't make it any worse than it is, before we even see what happens. Usually, things aren't as bad as they seem."

"I just hope you're right, Carlotta, but be careful anyway."

"Hmmm." Pensively she watched the old man walk away until he disappeared into the stable.

* * *

As was her habit, Carlotta returned to her kitchen after the afternoon horse feeding at Mercy Ranch. She was just making herself a second cup of coffee when the phone rang.

"Mancini here," she said pleasantly, but when she heard the voice on the other end of the line her tone hardened.

"Well, Mr. Pendleton. Do you have a problem with short-term memory? I seem to remember that only a few days ago I told you and Mayor Gates that I will never sell Mercy Ranch. And my decision is final. If you would be so kind as to respect it, I would be grateful."

88

But Mr. Pendleton pressed on, still trying to convince Carlotta of the wisdom of selling her ranch.

"I've already come to an agreement with most of the farmers in town. You know that I would pay more for your ranch than it's worth. Maybe you should reconsider."

Carlotta got angry and accidentally knocked over her coffee cup, spilling its contents onto the countertop and into the sink.

"My dear Mr. Pendleton, further efforts on your part to convince me to sell will be futile. I'll say it again, Mercy Ranch is not for sale – at any price. I have to end our little chat now because of a small emergency here. Have a nice day, and please don't call me again." With these words, she put the phone to one side and dedicated herself to cleaning up the spilled coffee.

With a disappointed sigh, Warren J. Pendleton hung up the receiver. It seemed that for the first time in his life he was going to have to accept defeat. He wasn't going to achieve his goal, at least not as he had pictured it. The Mancini woman wasn't going to budge from her decision not to sell.

Then his glance fell on Nancy's note, which he had found last evening when he returned home. It still lay on the little table next to the phone.

Warren: Beth and I have gone to visit Rondo. It wasn't right for you to sell the horse. Our daughter is unhappy, and I am too. Our family is being destroyed because all you live for is your work. I need a few days to myself to think things over. – Nancy

Pendleton rubbed his hand across his eyes. He'd been too tired last night to give much thought to what his wife had written. But now, in the cold light of day, her meaning finally got through to him.

Slowly he looked around and noticed, for the first time, that in the two days they had lived here, Nancy had made the new house very cozy, and he hadn't even been aware of it until now.

Haven't I done everything to give my family a comfortable life? he rationalized to himself. He had to admit, however, that he couldn't remember the last time he, Nancy, and Beth had spent any time together as a family. And what else had his wife written? *Beth is unhappy.*

Pendleton dropped down onto a kitchen chair. *Why are all these problems coming at me at once?* For a long time, he sat and stared into space.

For Nancy and Beth, the traffic light is yellow, he murmured to himself. *And it's up to me to determine whether it turns green or red! I've been a blind fool.*

* * *

As they did every school morning, Ricki and her friends greeted one another at the bike stand in front of school.

"Where's Beth? She said was going to meet us here," Cathy asked, trying to find the new student in the crowd of high school kids.

"Maybe she's already inside. She might have wanted to get acquainted with the place."

"Yeah, that's possible. Hey, I have great news for you

guys!" Ricki burst out. She was just about to begin her story when she spotted Ms. Murphy, who was hurrying toward the door. Suddenly she remembered the grammar test *the Murph* had promised to give the class this morning.

"Oh, no!" the girl exclaimed. "I forgot to study for the test!"

Cathy and Lillian grinned, and Kevin wisecracked, "Alert the media! Ricki forgot to study. Who are you trying to kid? It's not like it's the first time, is it?"

Slowly, the kids walked toward the school. *How could I have been such an idiot last night and forgotten about this test?* Ricki asked herself. Then she remembered her conversation with Gwen. It had been so exciting, so filled with possibilities, that it drove everything else from her mind.

* * *

As the stable where Rondo was being boarded came into view, Beth, beside herself with excitement, tortured her mother with endless unanswerable questions: "Do you think he'll recognize me? Do you think he's okay? What are we going to do if someone is out riding him?"

"I'm sure he'll still know you," Nancy tried to comfort her daughter, but the fact that her daughter was getting quieter by the minute began to bother her. Maybe it had been unwise to come back to their old town with Beth so soon, while the pain of her loss was still so fresh. On the other hand, Nancy reasoned, perhaps Beth would be able to handle the loss better – get some closure – if she could see that the animal was in good hands. She would finally have the chance to say good-bye to Rondo, which she had been deprived of by her father's abrupt action.

91

"Okay then, let's go!" Nancy said after she had parked the Jeep.

Beth nodded tensely as she got out of the vehicle. She had been here so often in the past for riding lessons. She knew every bush, every tree by heart, and she could have walked to Rondo's stall blindfolded.

"Beth, are you coming?" Nancy held the door to the riding hall open for her daughter, and Beth now entered with a heavy heart. As luck would have it, she ran into her former riding instructor, who was just leaving the tack room.

"Well, look who's here!" Chad Cameron exclaimed, very happy to see her. "I never expected to see you, Beth, or your wonderful mother! Did you miss Rondo so much, or did you just miss me?" He tried to keep the conversation as light as possible. He had to find a way to prepare the girl for the current condition of her former horse.

Beth forced a pleasant smile.

"Hello, Mr. Cameron. I had to find out how my horse, well, I mean my *old* horse, is doing."

"In this stable, every horse does well!" Cameron boasted. "But, well... at the moment, Rondo... how can I say this... is a little under the weather."

Beth was shocked. "What do you mean, 'under the weather'?" she wanted to know. "Is he sick?"

"Well, not exactly," the riding instructor began. But before he could continue, Beth, her heart beating wildly, was on her way to her beloved Rondo's stall. *Please, let him be okay!*

Nancy slowly followed behind her daughter with Chad Cameron,

"What's wrong with Rondo?" she asked seriously.

Cameron shook his head slowly. "Well, nothing physically. He's sound in wind and limb, as the saying goes. But over the past few weeks he's become completely apathetic, listless, and unresponsive when people approach or try to talk to him. He just stands in his stall, resigned, and refuses to eat."

Nancy looked at him out of the corner of her eye. "Chad, I don't know much about horses – well, actually, I know nothing at all. But if these same symptoms were found in humans, the diagnosis would be severe depression. What can be done to lift him out of his lethargy?"

"For most horses, it's enough if they're distracted and have something to do, but in Rondo's case –"

"What do you mean, 'in Rondo's case'?"

"Well, the new owner, Cass..."

"Please, get to the point."

"Okay, this is the situation. After the riding accident that caused the death of her first horse, Ashanti, Cass felt responsible, and her fear of horses became crippling. Just being around them was more than she could handle. Her parents hoped that with Rondo, a gentler, more reliable animal, she'd be able to get over her fear. She tried, but she didn't make it, and she never comes to the stable anymore. The Meyers never should have bought her that horse."

Nancy began to walk faster. She needed to be with her daughter. She didn't even dare think of what was going through Beth's head right now.

A few feet away from Rondo's stall she could hear Beth crying softly. The girl was standing beside her horse, her arms around his neck.

Rondo had scarcely looked up when the girl whispered his name, but his gaze spoke volumes. *Why did you abandon me?*

In a quaking voice Beth turned to her mother and said, "I knew he wasn't doing well! I could feel it! Cass doesn't love him. I know it, and he knows it too! Just look at his coat. I'm sure she hasn't groomed him lately, and I doubt she's even been here to visit him. Oh, Mom, I hate her! And... and... I hate my father because of this! It's his fault that Rondo is so sad! I don't want to have anything to do with him ever again!" Her last words sounded almost hysterical and Rondo stepped weakly aside. Why couldn't people just leave him alone? The time when he had hoped Beth would come back was over. It was too late.

Nancy stared at her daughter.

It hurt her so much to see her daughter's pain over Rondo's condition, and she felt furious with her husband, too. On the other hand, she was angry with herself as well. It had been a mistake to come here. Beth would be even sadder now that she had seen her horse.

"I think it would be better if we left," she said softly.

"I'm not leaving here until Rondo feels better!" Beth said, determined.

"What are you thinking? You can't stay here, and you know that!"

"I'm going to do it anyway, and no one can stop me!"

"Chad, the phone!" someone yelled across the corridor. Cameron waved to show that he had heard.

"Please, don't go anywhere. I'll be right back," he said quickly to Beth's mother before rushing off and disappearing into the office.

* * *

"How'd you do on that grammar test?" Lillian called out to Ricki when the school day was over and they were meeting at their usual place.

"Not too bad, I think," responded Ricki. "Thanks for asking."

"How come Beth isn't with you? Wasn't she in class?"

Ricki shook her head. "No. Maybe we misunderstood, and she's not coming until tomorrow."

"No way! We didn't misunderstand anything."

"Hmmm. It's a mystery! Maybe she got sick," Cathy suggested.

"She looked fine yesterday."

Kevin nodded. "Oh, I just remembered. Ricki, weren't you about to tell us some news this morning before you got spooked by the Murph?"

Ricki hit her forehead with the palm of her hand.

"Of course! It's the reason I forgot about the test in the first place. Listen to this! Gwen called me last night; well, actually, I called her, but whatever. At any rate, we talked for a long time, and get this," the girl paused dramatically before continuing. "Just imagine, Gwen complained to her grandmother that she hadn't seen us in ages and that she'd love to see us again, and she said she was sure we wouldn't mind being around the teenage guest riders at Highland Farms Estate. She told her grandmother that we already have some experience dealing with guests at Carlotta's ranch this winter, and –"

"Girlfriend, give us the bottom line already!" Cathy interrupted her friend.

"Let her finish!" Lillian was bursting with curiosity.

Ricki laughed. "Exactly, let me finish!"

"Then finish!"

"Then stop interrupting me! Be quiet and let me finish my story. I can tell you this: It has a happy ending."

Ricki's little speech had an immediate effect. With a nod to Cathy, she said, "The bottom line is this: We've been invited to spend a week at Highland Farms during summer vacation, and, of course, we can bring our horses! Can you believe it?" The girl smiled broadly.

"Wow!"

"Totally cool!"

"Incredible!"

Ricki nodded in agreement.

"You can imagine how excited I was last night when Gwen told me. Now you can understand why I completely forgot about the grammar test."

Kevin nodded supportively. "Who cares about grammar?" he asked, winking.

"You dope!" Ricki grinned. After the kids had calmed down a little, they got on their bikes and rode home, but not before they made sure that they all were getting together that afternoon.

"We have to ride over to Carlotta's today and tell her the good news," commented Cathy.

"Yeah, and more! I'm supposed to say hello from Mrs. Highland, and tell her that it's time for the two of them to get together again," Ricki added, laughing.

"She'll be glad to hear that. Let's get going. The sooner we get home, the sooner we can go riding." Lillian winked cheerily to the others and then she started pedaling as fast as she could. The thought of going riding that afternoon spurred her on to her best bike pedaling performance, and soon the others were yards behind her.

Where does she get her strength? Ricki asked herself, panting after a few minutes.

* * *

Warren Pendleton had tried several times to reach his wife on her cell phone, but apparently Nancy had turned it off.

"Too bad," he regretted, but then a smile spread over his face. At least this way he would *see* Beth's and her mother's reactions to what he was going to say to them when they returned.

He was about to put his cell phone in his jacket pocket, but decided to write Nancy a text message instead.

I miss you. Everything's going to be all right. I'm looking forward to your return. Say hi to Beth. – Warren

With a feeling of satisfaction, something that he hadn't felt in a long, long time, he left the house. He wanted to call on Mrs. Mancini personally one last time.

Chapter 7

Back at Ricki's house, after they had dropped off their books and changed into their riding gear at their own homes, the kids continued their excited chatter about the upcoming summer visit to Highland Farms Estate. Then they mounted their horses for their afternoon ride.

"I can't tell you guys how happy I am!" Cathy chirped as she rocked back and forth in Rashid's saddle.

"Cathy, sit still. You're going to drive Rashid crazy with all that rocking!" Lillian, who rarely missed an opportunity to scold her younger friend, shook her head, a little annoyed.

"Well, I feel like I just won the lottery!" Kevin admitted. "After all, we've been dreaming of spending time at the estate for weeks!"

"That's true. So, what are you saying, Kevin, that dreams can come true?" asked Ricki, and then she was reminded of Beth and Rondo.

"Do you guys think Beth will get to see her horse again?" she asked out of the blue.

"Huh? What made you think of that right now?"

"You know, because of dreams that can come true."

"Oh! I don't know, but I hope so for her sake. I think she's really nice," responded Lillian, pensively.

"Yes, she is, but listen, people, I need a gallop! Does anyone have a problem with that?" Cathy looked at each of them, and a short glance was enough to see that they all agreed. Without another word, the kids let their horses race down the forest trail.

The horses kept springing over imaginary shadow obstacles that were thrown across the path by the trees. The kids bent down low over their horses' necks and enjoyed the wonderful feeling of lightness with which the horses moved.

As always, they were caught up in a feeling of joy, a sort of ecstasy that people who ride experience when they hear the drumming of the hooves beneath them. The kids all agreed there was nothing better than this, and enjoyed every second of the spirited ride as though it were their last gallop.

As they reached the end of the trail, they slowed their horses, and while the animals got their breathing back to normal with a few isolated snorts, the kids' eyes shone brighter than on Christmas day.

"That was fabulous!" Kevin exclaimed. He leaned forward as far as he could and wrapped his arms around Sharazan's neck enthusiastically. The girls didn't hold back their praise for their horses either. Then they rode on in silence, not wanting to disturb the magic of that moment of indescribable happiness with words.

After a well-paced trot, they reached Mercy Ranch, and as they rode into the yard Kevin broke into a wild, exuberant yelp when he saw the cool sports car parked there. Carlotta's old Mercedes looked like an antique next to it.

"Wow, that is some machine! Who do we know who can afford a car like that?" Fascinated, he rode up closer to the car.

"Be careful that Sharazan doesn't suddenly ram into it," Ricki warned her boyfriend.

"It's definitely a custom job. What an amazing set of wheels! And look at the paint job. Man, this car is awesome!"

"Sharazan, be careful your owner doesn't decide to trade you in for some shiny piece of metal!" called Lillian, laughing, and received an angry look from the boy.

"This isn't just some piece of metal! It's a Porsche!"

Kevin rolled his eyes and then, with difficulty, he turned his attention away from the car to follow the girls into the stable to Carlotta's guest stalls, where they always put their horses when they visited.

As they led their horses along the corridor they ran into Kieran, Hal, Lena, and Cheryl, who were talking with one another, serious expressions on their faces.

"Hey!" Cathy called out cheerily when she saw Hal, overjoyed to see her boyfriend. She tried to give him a quick kiss on the cheek, and was a little surprised when the boy gave her just a weak smile and took a step backward, embarrassed.

"Is something wrong?" she asked, perplexed, but Hal just shook his head. He exchanged a short glance with Lena, but Cathy didn't notice.

"How are you?" Kevin asked.

"Hi," was all that Carlotta's stall helpers could muster.

"Hey, what happened to you guys?" Lillian stopped in front of the wooden bench with Holli and looked at the other young people curiously. "There's something wrong, I can tell. Did something happen?"

"Not yet," answered Kieran in a sad voice. "But a little while ago a guy arrived..."

"Oh, then that cool Porsche in the driveway must belong to him."

"Yeah, exactly. And we know from Carlotta that he's the developer who wants to buy the ranch."

"Oh," replied Ricki lazily. "And that's why you guys are all in a bad mood? Carlotta told us yesterday that she wouldn't sell the ranch under any conditions. That developer wants to build a hotel here, along with a golf course, but without Carlotta's approval the project can't go through."

"I don't know about that. We sorta listened in, and we heard Carlotta say to him, 'Then we're agreed.'"

Lillian looked at Kieran, shaking her head.

"There's no way Carlotta would gave in. If it were anybody else, it would be possible, but not Carlotta. Not when her horses are involved!"

As they spoke, the kids unsaddled their horses and led them into the guest stalls.

Cathy, who had finished getting Rashid settled in first, ran over to Hal for a hug, but her boyfriend pushed her away and mumbled something like, "I'm not in the mood today."

"Fabulous!" The disappointment over Hal's rejection was visible on her face, but somehow the girl could understand that his thoughts at the moment were more with the ranch than with her. After all, Carlotta's stable had become almost a second home for Hal and his friends, a place where the kids spent almost all of their free time.

"Psssst... they're coming!" Kieran whispered suddenly as he pointed out the window.

"I can't wait to hear what's going on," whispered Lena in response, and then she and the other kids pretended to be busy in the stalls. After all, they didn't want to appear too anxious. Quickly, Lena went over to Hal and started to help him untangle Jonah's mane, and while doing so she kept touching the boy's hand, as if by accident.

"When are you going to tell her?" Lena asked Hal softly. Hal just shrugged his shoulders.

"You have to tell her!" the girl insisted.

"I know, but I don't know how!"

Lena made an angry face. "How do you think? You just tell her that it's over between you two!"

Hal shook his head barely visibly. "It's not that simple."

"I thought you cared about me!"

"Yeah, I do, but I like Cathy, too, and – Oh, it's just such a mess!"

Lena's look hurled sparks, but when she realized that

Cathy was watching them her expression turned as soft as butter and she put her hand demonstrably on Hal's shoulder.

"I understand you," she said, her voice like velvet. "But you can only have one girlfriend, so you have to decide."

"I already decided," answered Hal. "But still, it's really hard for me to tell Cathy. She –" He stopped talking as Carlotta and the developer entered the stable.

Warren J. Pendleton nodded pleasantly to the young people, and he didn't seem to notice that they responded very hesitantly.

Cathy, who felt sick at the thought of Carlotta selling the ranch, only picked up a little of what was going on, as the owner of Mercy Ranch walked the potential buyer through the stable and showed him everything in detail. The kids could hardly believe that Carlotta was explaining to the developer, with a wink, that the tack room was entirely too small for a golfer's café, but Cathy only had eyes for Hal.

She stared at her boyfriend, incredulous that he was allowing the annoying Lena to get close to him like that. Usually Lena got on everyone's nerves with her constant complaints and put-downs. So, who did she think she was, acting like that with Hal right in front of Cathy? Didn't Lena know that Cathy and Hal were a couple?

When Carlotta and Mr. Pendleton had disappeared again into the house after a long walk around the stable, Cathy ran right over to Jonah's stall.

"What's going on?" she asked hoarsely and stared at Hal. She tried to ignore Lena.

"What do you mean?" asked Lena with a fake smile. Hal didn't feel comfortable with the situation at all and let her answer for him.

"Would you please stay out of this?" Cathy yelled at her, "I didn't ask you!"

"It's time to tell her, sweetheart!" Lena trilled and Cathy groaned.

Slowly, Hal turned around and had a terrible time looking into Cathy's eyes.

"I'm sorry," he said softly, and the girl knew immediately that her hopes of having him as a long-term boyfriend were destroyed. "I wanted to tell you alone..."

Cathy felt her heart cramp with pain, and hot tears filled her eyes. "Why?" she whispered, choked up. "Please tell me why. I thought we were happy."

Hal swallowed hard. "We were happy, but I... well, Lena and I... we..." he stammered helplessly, unable to finish the sentence.

Cathy understood. She gave the two of them a long look that almost broke Hal's heart.

"Why Lena?" the girl asked hesitantly. "Of all the girls, why *her*?"

But since she didn't get any answer, she turned slowly and walked directly into Rashid's stall. As if in a trance, she began to saddle her foster horse. She just wanted to get away – away from the ranch and away from Hal who, by leaving her for Lena, had hurt her more than any one else in her life.

Lillian, who had witnessed only some of the encounter between the three teens, saw Cathy saddling her horse and ran over to her.

"Cathy, what's wrong? Did all that talk about the golfer's café get you upset? You know Carlotta wasn't being serious, don't you?" Suddenly she stopped short. "Hey, what is it? Come on, tell me!"

All of a sudden Cathy felt weak, and she leaned against Rashid's neck, crying softly to herself.

"It's over..." she said, barely audible.

"What?" Lillian didn't know what she meant.

"He... he broke up with me... because of... because of Lena."

"Lena? You can't be serious!"

Cathy just wasn't able to give her friend an answer. Awkwardly, she fumbled around, trying to buckle the snaffle, as though it were the first time she had ever done it.

Lillian was silent for a moment, but then she shook her head firmly. "And now you want to go home, don't you?"

Cathy nodded.

"So you want to let Lena enjoy the victory of stealing your boyfriend? Listen, if he thinks he can treat you like that, then he isn't worth a single tear!"

Cathy spun around. "And what do you think I should do? Wish them both luck?"

"Only if it helps you. But there's one thing you shouldn't do – and that's hang your head and let her take over."

"I can't stay. Not now!"

"Yes, you can!" Lillian went into Rashid's stall, grabbed

Cathy by the shoulders and shook her gently. "You're not leaving now! You're going to show Hal that you don't need him. Lena's not going to drive you away!"

"I can't!" repeated Cathy piteously, but Lillian remained stubborn and began undoing the saddle girth.

"Then just act as if you can! Don't you get it, Cathy? This is just what Lena wants! She's probably afraid that Hal will go back to you if you stick around the ranch."

Cathy didn't know what she should think anymore, let alone what she should do. Incapable of making a decision, she stood in front of Rashid and forced herself not to keep looking over at Hal and Lena.

Lena was laughing loudly, and now she gave Hal a hug. It was obvious that he didn't feel comfortable with the situation.

"That rat!" Cathy's despair began to turn into anger. "She doesn't like him the way I do!"

"Well, if that's true, then he's going to notice it sooner or later, and then he's really going to feel bad!" Lillian put the saddle back down in front of the stall.

"Do you think he'll come back to me some day?" asked Cathy suddenly.

"I don't know," Lillian answered slowly. "But I'm not so sure that would be a good thing."

"Hmmm."

The sixteen-year-old put her arms around her friend.

"There's no sense thinking about it right now. Come on, Cathy. Let's get the grooming equipment for Jam and

Sheila. The two of them look awful. They must have rolled around in a big pile of mud!"

* * *

Nancy Pendleton had finally convinced Beth to say good-bye to Rondo and leave the stable with her, but only after she promised her daughter, on her word of honor, that they would come back the next day.

"I have some things to think over, Beth, but I can't do it here," Nancy had argued, but actually, she was already considering how she could convince her husband to buy back Rondo. Clearly, in light of the present situation with Cass, Meyers would not be against such an arrangement.

Of course, Nancy would have preferred talking to Beth about it, but she didn't want to raise her daughter's hopes only to see them dashed if Warren wouldn't agree.

Now the two of them were on their way to a small Bed and Breakfast where they were staying overnight. Since they hadn't waited in the stable for Chad Cameron to return, Nancy didn't know that Mr. Meyers had called the riding instructor to tell him that he had finally found a buyer for Rondo.

* * *

After Carlotta said a friendly good-bye to the developer, she hurried back to the stable, where the kids received her with mixed emotions.

"What's wrong?" she asked, although she knew precisely what her young helpers were thinking.

"That guy acted like he got exactly what he wanted," replied Kieran, his voice raw.

"That's true!" Carlotta nodded.

"So that means..." Kevin didn't finish his sentence, but each of them knew what he was going to ask.

"So he got to you! Wow, Carlotta, I never thought you'd give in!" Lillian's voice sounded reproachful, and incomprehension was reflected on all the kids' faces.

"Oh, he didn't have to try that hard to persuade me," teased Carlotta. "The offer he made me was just too tempting. I couldn't turn it down!"

"Great. We all thought you'd never sell the ranch." Finally, Carlotta laughed out loud.

"Well, I guess it's time to clear up this misunderstanding," she said and pounded the ground with her crutch. She looked from one kid to the other with affection. "You don't really think that I sold my Mercy Ranch, do you?"

The kids turned red and looked down at the ground.

"Of course we talked about it, but the man understood pretty quickly that there was no way that I was going to sell, no matter what kind of financial offer he made me."

"So you didn't sell?"

"Of course not. Do I look like the kind of person who would throw away a life's dream for a few dollars?" Carlotta grinned. She was glad to see the happiness back in the eyes of her young friends.

"Phew, I am so glad!" Kieran breathed a sigh of relief.

"I thought I was going to have to say good-bye to the best part of my day! That would have been awful!"

"But then, what kind of an offer did the developer make?" Ricki asked. Carlotta just shook her head.

"You're going to find that out soon enough, my dears!" she said, winking. Then she looked around.

"Where are Hal and Lena? Weren't the two of them here a while ago?" she asked, surprised.

Cathy pressed her lips together and tried not to look at Carlotta.

Lillian took a deep breath. "Well, the two of them had some plans, I guess," she responded vaguely. She didn't say that Lena had managed to steer Hal away, since Cathy hadn't left as she had expected her to do.

"Oh, okay." Carlotta turned to go. "I have a few things I have to attend to. If you have nothing else to do, you could take care of the snaffles and saddles. It wouldn't hurt for them to be rubbed with some oil."

"Yes, ma'am!" saluted Kieran and grinned happily at Carlotta. He was so glad the ranch hadn't been sold.

* * *

"Did you spray Diablo's scrape wound again?" Jake questioned Ricki in the early evening, when the kids were back in the Sulais' stable.

"Of course."

"And, Lillian, did you remember to get the worm medicine for the horses from the vet? You were going to do it last week."

The girl groaned. "Oh, no, I totally forgot! I'm sorry, Jake. In the last few days, there's been so much going on. First, they kept changing the schedule for the afternoon classes, and then I had to –"

"No excuses! You don't have to apologize to me. After all, they're your horses, and it's about their health." Jake said with emphasis.

Lillian rolled her eyes. "Yeah, I know. I'll go over to the vet tomorrow and get the stuff. I promise!"

"Well, see that you do!" Jake was in a rare mood. "By the way, Kevin, did you notice that Sharazan's licking stone is all gone? Please, get him a new one. They contain important minerals that are good for the horses. Sometimes I have the impression that these things don't interest you, and that all you want to do is ride!"

Kevin stopped brushing his horse and peered over his roan's back toward the groom.

"Boy, Jake, you sure are in a bad mood today! You know these horses mean everything to us."

"Really? Sometimes I doubt that. And Cathy... even though Rashid doesn't belong to you, you should make sure that his gate is closed. Last night the latch wasn't shut. Life isn't just about love, and instead of always thinking about Hal, maybe you should –"

The girl inhaled sharply and gave Jake an angry look. She threw the rubber grooming comb on the ground and ran outside. Rashid, who was still tied up in the corridor, was startled by the sudden movement and, looking confused, watched her leave.

"And before you run out feeling insulted, you could put your horse back in the stall and return the grooming equipment to the tack room," Jake called out nastily.

"That was really mean of you, Jake," said Ricki, softly. "Hal broke up with Cathy today and she's really upset!"

For a moment, the old man looked embarrassed, but then he stuck out his chin stubbornly. "Sorry to hear it, but that's no excuse for neglecting your horses!" With a look of annoyance, the old groom walked out of the stable.

The three teens were puzzled.

"Was there a full moon last night? What's going on? I've never seen him like this before," commented Kevin.

"I have," responded Ricki with a sigh. "Sometimes he can be impossible."

"On the other hand, he's right," Lillian replied. "At least as far as I'm concerned. But the way he treated Cathy wasn't right. After all, he knows Rashid can open the latch himself, no matter how tight you push it in. He always manages to get out of his stall."

"That's true. Where did Cathy go?" Ricki went to the doorway, and looked around. "Uh-oh, she's over there with Rosie, crying into her fur. I wonder if I should –"

Lillian held her back. "Leave her alone. Right now, I think your dog is more of a comfort for her than you are. She just listens to Cathy instead of saying all kinds of silly stuff that might not help anyway."

"Hmmm. I guess you're right."

Kevin brought Sharazan to his stall and then put Rashid

in his. He paid special attention to the latch, making sure that it was closed tightly.

"Well, I would never have thought that Hal would be interested in Lena," Kevin commented

"Oh, please! I don't want to know how much she flirted and what she told him to make him drop Cathy. I think that was really low of him," his girlfriend responded.

"Men!" Lillian looked at Ricki.

Kevin just made a face but didn't say anything. Sometimes he wasn't exactly proud to be a guy. On the other hand, he knew there were plenty of girls who could be unbelievably nasty, and Lena was one of them.

"By the way, we have to visit Carlotta tomorrow. My father's bringing over a load of hay and we're supposed to help unload it," Lillian remembered all of a sudden.

"Hay disappears almost instantly at Mercy Ranch," said Ricki. "But no wonder, with so many horses."

"Sometimes I wonder how Carlotta pays for all of it. Maybe she has a secret sponsor," said Kevin.

"Oh, I wish I had a secret sponsor, or even a secretive one, who would add to my allowance every week," grinned Ricki.

"I wouldn't say no to that either, but it's not going to happen." Kevin said.

"I've been thinking about looking for a job... shelving stuff at the supermarket or something like that, in order to have a little more spending money," said Lillian. "But it's all a question of time. In the morning and early afternoon I have school, then I go riding with Holli, and then I have homework and studying to do in the evenings. If I don't do it then, I'll never have time to study, and my parents would kill me if my grades were lower than average. So when do I have time for a job? It's totally lousy, and I could really use a few more dollars," she sighed.

"Who couldn't?"

The kids tidied up their grooming equipment and put it all away in the tack room before going outside. Cathy came toward them, her eyes red and swollen from crying.

"I'm sorry I ran off," she said quietly. "I have to get Rashid –"

"I already did it," Kevin nodded to her with a smile.

Cathy swallowed hard. "Thanks... I'm going home now. I don't feel like doing anything more today anyway. See you all later."

"Okay, see you tomorrow, and try not to think about Hal too much!" Lillian called after her. She knew, however, that for the next few days, Cathy's thoughts would be all about Hal.

Chapter 8

Back at the Bed and Breakfast where they were staying, it took Nancy a long time to calm Beth down after the excitement of the day. When the girl finally fell asleep, Nancy turned on her cell phone, surprised to see a text message from Warren. As she read it, a warm smile animated her face. The trip had worked. *"Everything's going to be all right,"* he wrote. Maybe now would be the right time to call him and talk about the possibility of buying Rondo back.

She called him on their home phone as well as on his cell phone, but both times she was unable to reach him.

"Darn it," Nancy murmured to herself after several attempts. Since her battery was getting low, she decided to try again first thing in the morning on the Bed and Breakfast pay phone downstairs.

"I'm sorry," the owner told her the next morning. "We had

a pretty bad storm a few days ago, and the telephone lines in this part of town are still down."

Nancy frowned unhappily. *Well,* she thought, *one day isn't going to make any difference. It's probably best if I talk with Warren about everything when we get back home.*

* * *

When Nancy returned to their room, Beth was sitting on her bed, dressed and ready to go.

"I thought you'd still be asleep."

The girl shook her head. "I had such terrible nightmares about Rondo last night that I'm glad to be awake. He got thinner and thinner, until he couldn't walk. There were a lot of strange people standing around him in the stall, and they just laughed when he fell over. I'm still upset about it." Beth rubbed her eyes.

"It was just a dream!" Nancy sat down beside her daughter and put her arm around her, trying to calm her down.

"Are we going to go see Rondo now?"

"It's still pretty early and I don't think there will be anyone at the stable yet."

Beth objected. "Someone has to be there. After all, the horses have to be fed."

Nancy smiled at the girl. "I'm hungry, too! If it's all right with you, let's have breakfast here before we leave."

Beth made a face. "Do we have to?"

Nancy nodded firmly. "Yes!"

With a heavy heart, Beth obeyed her mother and

followed her to the inn's little dining room. A table set with a bouquet of flowers, fresh muffins, and fresh-squeezed orange juice awaited them.

"Do you think Rondo ate something yesterday?" Beth asked, glancing at the baked goods.

"I don't know," Nancy admitted honestly. She would have loved to say something comforting to her daughter, but after everything that Chad Cameron had told her yesterday, it didn't look good for Rondo.

Beth slid back and forth restlessly on her chair, and she almost tore the tablecloth off the table when she jumped up as soon as Nancy was finished with breakfast.

The last half hour had seemed like an eternity to the girl, and she was happy to be sitting next to her mother in the Jeep a short time later.

"Oh no, there's so much traffic today!" she groaned impatiently as Nancy had to stop at yet another red light. "Could we buy some carrots or some apples in a supermarket somewhere? Rondo used to like them so much. Maybe that would stimulate his appetite."

"It's worth a try," Nancy said and soon steered the car toward a supermarket parking lot.

About twenty minutes later, she stopped the SUV in front of the riding stable and waited for Beth to get out. Her daughter, however, remained in her seat, bent over and pressing the bag of apples close to her chest.

"I don't feel well," she said quietly, her face pale. "I'm so afraid for Rondo and I have such a guilty conscience about him. I shouldn't have allowed him to be sold. It's my fault that he's sick now."

Nancy took a deep breath. "Now listen closely, Beth. Nothing is your fault. No one could have known that Cass wouldn't take care of him, and I'm sure your father wouldn't have sold him to Mr. Meyers if he had known that Rondo was going to be neglected."

"He would have sold him to anyone who had the money to buy him!" Beth answered bitterly.

"That's not true!"

"Yes, it is!"

Nancy was silent for a moment and looked pensively at her daughter.

"Come on, let's go inside. I'm sure Rondo will be glad to get the apples," she said softly. Beth stared into the distance, and then she nodded vaguely and finally got out of the car. When she realized she was only going to be able to spend a short time with her beloved horse and then she would have to leave him again, she felt like crying.

"Good morning, ladies!" Noah Hickson, the groom, greeted them warmly. He was just coming out of the feed storage room. "To what do I owe the pleasure of this early-morning visit?"

"How's Rondo?" the girl burst out, not even saying hello. "Has he eaten anything?"

Hickson's glance fell on the apples. "You... brought him a treat?" he replied, avoiding Beth's question.

"Yes! I'm going to –" Beth started to leave but Hickson held her back.

"Stay here," he said softly, and Nancy sensed something had happened that was going to hurt Beth terribly.

"Rondo... well, he... he's not here anymore."

Beth turned as pale as a ghost. "What? Not here anymore?" She feared the worst. "Is he... is he... dead?"

Hickson shook his head and smiled compassionately. "No, of course he's not dead. But he was sold yesterday and was transported to his new home this morning, just before you got here. I'm so sorry, Beth, that you weren't able to say good-bye to him."

"Oh, no!" the girl whispered as her eyes filled with tears. "Do you know where they took him? I mean, do you have an address?"

"No, unfortunately not." Hickson watched sadly as Nancy wrapped her arms around Beth. If there was anything that made him feel helpless, it was seeing women cry.

Embarrassed, he turned away. He could imagine how awful it must be for Beth, but Beth didn't even notice him.

Rondo was gone! Forever! She would never see him again. She wouldn't even know if he was with loving people who would take good care of him. Oh, it was all so horrible!

Nancy bit her lip. Why hadn't she tried to reach Warren yesterday afternoon, when the thought first crossed her mind?

She stroked Beth's hair gently. "Come, let's go. There's nothing more we can do here," she said hoarsely, and led Beth back to the car.

"Yes, Mom, let's go home. I can't stand to be here any longer. Everything reminds me of Rondo."

Nancy nodded sympathetically. "It's okay, sweetheart," she answered softly. Then she steered the Jeep toward the highway that would take them back home.

* * *

Carlotta stood in front of the paddock, observing the horses. It always gave her such pleasure to see how contented the herd of veterans was. Slowly the animals moved forward, their heads low and their nostrils sunk in fresh sweet-smelling grass.

Carlotta leaned on the paddock fence and glanced at her watch. It was 3:30. Within the next few minutes her stable helpers would probably show up at the ranch.

She was just about to turn around to walk back to the stable when she noticed Dave Bates's old tractor, rattling noisily toward the ranch, pulling a trailer full of hay.

She looked toward him in surprise, her hands on her waist.

"Well," she called to him, "I guess I'm getting so senile that I can't remember ordering hay from you."

Lillian's father grinned. "I have the same problem," he answered laughing. "I was so forgetful today that I forgot how to write out a bill for hay!"

"And what does that mean exactly?" Carlotta wanted to know, her eyes wide.

"Very simple. Lillian thinks that Mercy Ranch needs to be supported and I happen to think that we have way too much hay stored in our barn. The fresh hay will be baled and brought in soon. Therefore, today's delivery comes *without* a bill!"

Carlotta shook her head.

"These kids are impossible! Lillian is going to bankrupt you if she continues like this, and if I counted up all of the things that I've gotten from you for free up till now... well, I'd probably have to get a part-time job just to pay off my debt. No, no, Dave, this won't do. You're going to write out a bill for this hay, or I'll have to ask you to turn around and take it right back home."

Mr. Bates looked up at the sky, as though Carlotta's protestations didn't concern him.

"You're out of luck, lady. I already had the work of loading it, and you don't think I'm going to unload all of this at home again, do you? Where are your helpers? Where do you want me to put the hay? In the barn or in the shed?"

Carlotta surrendered.

"The barn would be great. My hay reserves are pretty much depleted. But I hope you have a little time. My crew isn't here yet, but they should show up soon... at least, I hope so!" she added.

"No problem," he said, and then he drove the tractor slowly toward the barn. A little later, Carlotta and Lillian's father were sitting in her kitchen enjoying a cup of coffee while they waited for the kids to arrive.

* * *

Beth had calmed down during the drive home. Of course, it was still very painful to know that she would never see Rondo again, but she had at least tried to tell herself that the new owners would do everything possible to improve his health.

Nancy had just turned onto the side street not far from their house, when Beth spotted her new schoolmates, riding their bikes along the road.

"Mom, can you let me out? Ricki and the others are up there. I'd like to talk to them for a while."

Nancy nodded. "Sure thing." She was glad that her daughter was looking forward to connecting with her new friends so soon, and was sure that Beth would get over the separation from Rondo quicker that way.

"See you later," she called to her daughter before driving the last few yards to their driveway.

"Hi," Beth shouted as she ran toward the astonished bike riders.

"Well, look who's here!" Kevin grinned as he brought his bike to a full stop.

"We were beginning to think you'd gotten lost," Ricki said. "We missed you at school."

Beth's face clouded over. "I visited Rondo."

"Really?"

Beth nodded sadly. "He wasn't doing well. No one was paying enough attention to him, and now he's been sold again and I don't know who bought him."

"Just a minute, that was a little too fast for me and also a little confusing," interrupted Lillian.

Kevin pointed to his watch. "People, we have to get going. We're already late!"

"Where are you going?" Beth asked quickly.

"Carlotta's getting a load of hay delivered and we want to

help her unload it," explained Cathy with a stony expression on her face. She wasn't comfortable with the idea of running into Hal again, but her friends had worked on her until she had finally given in and agreed to go to the ranch.

"Oh," responded Beth, and without thinking it over, she said, "If you wait here for me, I'll run home, get my bike, and come with you. And I can tell you all what happened on the way."

"Great," answered Ricki. "Do you live far from here?"

"No," Beth shook her head. "I live right over there. I'll be back in five minutes." Beth turned on her heel and ran down the street and into the driveway, and then disappeared into the garage.

"Wow!" exclaimed Cathy admiringly, looking at the handsome old houses that lined the street. "If Beth moved in there ... well, her father must be pretty rich!"

Lillian nodded. "I think we'll have to take a closer look sometime," she grinned with a wink.

True to her word, five minutes later Beth returned on her bike.

"Let's get going," she called, and the five rode off down the street.

"So tell us about your visit to Rondo," Ricki said.

"Okay," Beth began slowly. She took a deep breath and then she told her new friends the whole unhappy story.

"That's harsh!" responded Kevin. "And it's such a shame that you couldn't find out who bought him."

Beth sighed. "That's true, but who knows, maybe it's

better this way. Maybe it would have been better not to visit him. I'm learning that it doesn't do any good to open up old wounds."

"Hmm. I think it depends on the situation. I think you can get over something only when you've dealt with it. Of course, that brings some pain with it," reflected Lillian.

"Whatever," replied Beth. "I've lost Rondo, but you know what they say: If a friendship breaks up, move on to new ones!" Somewhat sadly, she looked over at Cathy, whose expression hardened immediately.

"Uh-oh, did I say something wrong?" Beth asked, upset.

"No," answered Cathy slowly. "It fits, since as of yesterday I'm solo again."

"Oh, gee, I'm really sorry! Do you want to talk about it?" she asked sympathetically.

"No, but I will." Cathy tried to grin and failed. "Maybe it'll help." So Beth heard the whole story about Cathy and Hal before the friends had turned into the ranch's yard.

"Darn, they're here!" Cathy whispered to Ricki when she saw Hal and Lena standing in front of the paddock.

"Be cool," replied Ricki. "Hey," she called out, especially friendly. "Everything okay?"

Lena turned her head away as though she hadn't heard Ricki.

Hal nodded and waved a little awkwardly, with a glance at Cathy. Kieran was the only one smiling broadly.

"It's great that you're here! Oh, and you brought some help," he said, seeing Beth. "That's terrific."

Lillian introduced their new friend to the others, and then looked around.

"Has my father arrived yet?" she asked Hal, but he just shrugged his shoulders.

"No idea. We just got here a few minutes ago and we haven't seen him."

Just then Carlotta and Mr. Bates came out of the house, and that answered Lillian's question.

"I could use this many helpers on my farm, too," Dave Bates commented.

"Then maybe you should change from cows to horses," Lillian suggested, but her father just laughed.

"No, no, otherwise I'd just take all these helpers from Carlotta's ranch, and that wouldn't do either."

"Oh, Mr. Bates, I don't think that would happen," interrupted Kieran. "After all, we can see that you're young and strong and totally able to take care of your farm yourself, whereas –"

"I'm old and decrepit and unable to get everything done on my own!" Carlotta finished his sentence, laughing.

"I didn't mean it that way," Kieran, embarrassed, tried to justify himself, but Carlotta gave him a warm smile.

"Don't worry about it, young man, I know what you meant!" Suddenly she noticed Beth and she smiled at her warmly. "Beth, it's a pleasure to see you here again. I thought perhaps you didn't like it here on my ranch, because you didn't come back."

"Oh, I love it here! There... there were other reasons why I didn't come. I... I wasn't home."

"Oh... well, it's nice to have you here anyway."

"I ran into Ricki and the others and heard that you were getting a load of hay, so I thought..."

Carlotta grinned. "You thought correctly. I'm glad for any help I can get." Then she clapped her hands. "The wagon is here and ready to be unloaded. If you hurry, there will be enough time to go riding afterward, if you want."

Kieran, Hal, and Lena looked at one another in delight.

Dave Bates turned around and started walking toward the tractor. "But first to work!" he called over his shoulder. Laughing, he nodded at Carlotta before indicating to the young people to follow him. Not twenty-five minutes later, the bales of hay were all stacked neatly in the barn.

* * *

Warren J. Pendleton put his arms around his wife and gazed at her for a long time.

"I really missed you! It's nice that you're back early."

Nancy nodded.

"It's because Rondo was sold yesterday."

"Oh, I thought it was because of me," laughed Warren.

"That too," his wife beamed at him, but then she turned serious. "Actually, I wanted to call you and ask if..."

"If what?"

Nancy thought it over a bit and then she shook her head.

"Oh, nothing." There was no sense in talking about Rondo anymore.

"Where's Beth, by the way?"

"She ran into her new friends on the way home and wanted to go with them to that ranch for old horses."

"Mercy Ranch?" asked Warren with interest.

Nancy stared at her husband in amazement. "Yes, that's what it's called. But how did you know?"

"Oh, I have some business with the owner right now. By the way, I have an appointment with her later. Would you like to go with me and take a look at the place where we're probably going to find our daughter in the future?"

Nancy was even more surprised. That he was involving her in his business dealings was something completely new. She was incredibly happy about it.

"Of course! If you'd like," she replied, her eyes beaming.

"Yes, I'd like. Otherwise, I wouldn't have asked!" Pendleton glanced at the clock. "If we start now we'll get there right on time!"

* * *

"How are you?" Hal asked awkwardly when he ran into Cathy in the tack room. She was cooling down a blister at the sink.

The girl stared at the stream of water. "Do you really care?"

"Yeah, I do!"

Cathy was silent.

"I didn't mean to hurt you," said Hal softly.

The girl laughed artificially. "How nice of you! How did you think I would feel when you dumped me? Did you think I would jump for joy?"

"Cathy, please..."

"Cathy, please. Cathy, please!" she mimicked him before she turned on him in a huff. "Just tell me one thing. Why *her*?"

Hal didn't say anything. How could he explain to Cathy why he had been attracted to Lena when he himself didn't know why?

Suddenly there was a commotion outside the tack room. Kieran's laugh could be heard loudly through the door, and it was only a matter of moments before it would be opened and the others would come in.

"Hal, where are you? Haaaal..." Lena's voice seared Cathy's heart and even Hal jumped noticeably.

"I hope you will be very, very happy with her!" Cathy pushed past her former boyfriend and ran out, almost bumping into her rival.

"Can't you watch where you're going?" complained Lena nastily, and threw Hal an angry look as he followed Cathy out of the tack room and into the stable corridor.

"What did she want from you?" she asked him in an accusatory tone.

"Nothing."

"You two were gone for a long time, considering it was nothing."

"Oh, leave me alone!" Hal hissed through tight lips. He wanted to go back to the stalls. Lena's jealousy was starting to get on his nerves.

The girl took a deep breath and was just about to make an appropriate response, but then she quickly decided on a different strategy.

She put her hand on Hal's arm, trying to make up with him.

"I'm sorry. It's just that I..." she began, but after a look from her boyfriend she stepped back.

"I'd like to be by myself for a few minutes," Hal said and quickly walked away.

That stupid Cathy! Lena thought, and stared down the corridor, where she saw her predecessor standing in front of Sheila's stall. *If you think you're going to get him back, you're sadly mistaken!* Determined, she ran directly toward her.

"Stay away from Hal," she hissed. "He doesn't want you anymore, so get used to it!"

"Get away from me!" Cathy responded testily, without taking her eyes off the mare. "I'm not interested in Hal anymore!" she said, although her heart was saying something completely different.

"If you don't care, then I have to wonder what you two were doing in the tack room all that time!" Lena just couldn't leave it alone.

"That's none of your business! But if you have to know, ask him!"

"Hal is my boyfriend now. So keep your hands off him in the future! Is that clear?"

Cathy turned around in a fury. "What do you want from me? Am I supposed to give you a signed deed or something? Get out of here!"

Lena's shoulders stiffened.

"If anyone is going to leave, then it's you. I've been here longer than you! You don't belong at Mercy Ranch!"

"LENA! That's enough!" Carlotta's voice thundered at

the girl. Lena hadn't even noticed that the ranch owner had approached and heard her whole exchange with Cathy.

"I still decide who can come and go on my ranch! And anyway, I'd like to ask you two to have your fights, whatever they're about, somewhere else. I want peace on my ranch. There's no room here for people who want to fight, so remember that, you two!" She looked at the two girls severely. Her words filled them with remorse, and they stared at the floor. "I hope I made myself clear!" Then, in a calm voice, as though nothing had happened, she continued, "Lena, I thought that you wanted to go riding with Kieran and Hal. If that's the case, then it's time for you to saddle your horse. Cathy, you could help me sort out the crate of new halters."

"Sure, I'll help." Breathing a sigh of relief, Cathy followed Carlotta, but when she passed Lena, the other girl stuck out her tongue at her and gave her a mean look that seemed to say, *You haven't seen anything yet. I will make sure that you don't show up here anymore!*

Ricki and Lillian, who had heard parts of the fight, just looked at each other. They both felt that a power struggle had begun between Cathy and Lena and that the ending was still uncertain.

"There's nothing worse than a jealous woman," commented Lillian, and then the two of them ran outside to talk the whole thing over with Beth and Kevin. They were sure that the peaceful days on the ranch were over, at least as long as Lena and Cathy were fighting over Hal.

Chapter 9

Cathy sighed with relief as she watched Hal, Kieran, and Lena, riding Hadrian, Silver, and Jam off the ranch grounds. "I couldn't have stood being around her for another second," she said to her friends, plopping down on the wooden bench outside the barn. "That girl really gets on my nerves!"

"There's no sense getting upset," responded Lillian. "It doesn't help."

"Exactly," agreed Kevin.

"It's easy for you guys to talk! Lillian, you've got Josh, and Kevin has Ricki. Everyone's happy. I'm the only one who's alone!"

"You shouldn't talk like that just because you and Hal broke up. After all, I'm sure you'll..."

"Oh, Lily, you sound just like my mother."

"And you're drowning in self-pity!" burst out Beth, who up to then had just listened silently.

"You're one to talk!" Cathy objected angrily. "Who's been whining for hours about Rondo? 'I miss him so much... I can't live without him... How will I ever forget him?' Maybe you should look at yourself, as far as self-pity is concerned, before you start criticizing me!"

"My feelings for Rondo are completely different," Beth defended herself.

"Maybe not," responded Ricki, trying to smooth things over. "After all, you're both dealing with the loss of someone you cherished."

"Nonsense like that won't bring either Hal or Rondo back!" said Cathy aggressively and dug a hole in the gravel with the tip of her boot.

"If you kids start being mean to each other, then nothing is going to change, except for the worse!" All of a sudden Carlotta was standing in front of the kids, leaning on her crutch and looking straight at them. "Many of life's experiences are painful, but there are at least as many that are wonderful. Unfortunately, we just take the good ones for granted and we complain about the bad ones, although they still have a lot to teach us in terms of valuable life lessons."

"But why is it always me?" asked Cathy plaintively.

"Did you ask yourself that when your friendship with Hal began? Or when I gave you Rashid to take care of?"

Cathy couldn't answer.

No one said a thing... but Carlotta knew she had everyone's attention. It was time for some simple truths.

"You all just have to learn to be grateful when you're

happy. Be aware of those moments and be glad that you're able to experience them. And when those times are over, you have to accept the new consequences, and realize that your life still holds a lot of joy. Don't *worry* about the future. Live in the moment instead, and be curious about the wonderful things that are *going* to happen to you in your life."

"That all sounds so simple, Carlotta," Beth said thoughtfully. "But how can I be happy about anything when my heart still belongs to what I've lost?"

A sad, understanding smile came on Carlotta's face. "The only time you lose something is when you forget it. As long as you have your memories stored in your heart, you will never really lose it. And that's the way life's supposed to be. You should always remember something happy you experienced, never in sadness, and you should always be aware that happiness sometimes comes in strange packages, sometimes indirectly, or even in a completely different form. The fact is happiness never turns away from us, even though we may feel that it does."

Cathy and Beth exchanged a quick glance out of the corners of their eyes.

Nice words, but they don't help us right now! was what they both seemed to be thinking.

Carlotta was about to say something else when Warren Pendleton's flashy car approached the ranch.

Beth looked at the car, at first surprised, and then she scowled.

"What's my father doing here? That's all I need right now!"

"Huh? The developer guy is your father?" Lillian looked at Beth in amazement.

"He's here on business," said Carlotta.

Beth laughed unpleasantly. "Oh, terrific! First he takes Rondo away from me and now he's here, the only place I thought I'd be safe from him!" Quickly she turned to her new friends. "Can we go into the stable? Or somewhere else? I don't want to see him."

Kevin nodded. "Of course! Hey, let's take the dogs for a walk. Gandalf and Lucky certainly won't mind," he grinned.

"Good idea! Let's get out of here."

Quickly, the kids ran toward the stable, where they thought Carlotta's dogs would be. They were out of sight by the time Mr. Pendleton stopped his Porsche in front of Carlotta. With a warm smile on his face, he got out of the car.

"Hello, Mrs. Mancini, may I introduce my wife?"

"Hello, Mrs. Pendleton! I'm so glad you came along. By the way, you have a very nice daughter."

"Where is she?" Warren looked around. "I thought I saw her as we drove up the road."

Carlotta pointed toward the stable. "She's gone to the stable with the other kids. She's still not over your having sold Rondo."

"Oh... " Disappointed, Warren lowered his gaze, and Nancy kept shifting her weight from one foot to the other.

"Yes, that... that is still bothering her quite a lot," she said softly, embarrassed that Carlotta apparently knew all about it.

There's no telling how awful Beth made her father look, Nancy thought dejectedly. However, Carlotta didn't seem to be that interested. She quickly offered Beth's parents a cup of coffee and then they all walked over to the house.

* * *

Ricki took a quick peek around the corner and then grinned at Beth. "All clear! They've gone into the house. Hey, was that your mother?"

Beth's eyes widened. "Who? Was there someone else there? I can't imagine she —"

"Yeah, a woman. Dark longish hair, jeans, yellow T-shirt."

"That's Mom! Now I really don't understand anything."

"I feel like that all the time," laughed Lillian, and then she pointed at the dogs. They were playing with Kevin, letting him come within a few feet of them, and then running off.

"How am I supposed to get your leashes on if you don't let me catch you?" the boy panted, completely out of breath. "Without leashes, you can't go for walks! When are you going to get that?"

Ricki laughed. "Wait, we'll help you. The best thing is to surround them, then we can grab them."

"That's what you think.... Watch out, Lillian, hold on to Gandalf!" Kevin shouted, but the dog had already run away, out of the stable and into the yard.

Lillian ran after him and then abruptly stopped outside. "Hey, there's a horse trailer coming!" she shouted loudly. "Do you guys know if Carlotta's getting a new old-timer?"

"What? No, she didn't say anything to me about it," Ricki answered. Immediately, the friends walked out of the stable and excitedly watched the transporter approach.

"I'm going to go tell Carlotta," Cathy announced, and she ran into the house. A moment later, she came back, followed by the three adults.

"Hello, Beth. So, we get to see you here after all!" laughed Warren Pendleton as he waved to his daughter. Beth, however only managed a soft, "Hey," and was glad when her father didn't say anything else to her.

"Well, now I'm curious," said Carlotta.

The trailer pulled into the yard and carefully stopped next to Mr. Pendleton's sports car. A young man jumped out of the driver's cab and called, "Hi! Is this the right place?"

Carlotta shrugged her shoulders. "It depends on where you want to go," she said. She walked over to him and talked with him quietly, making it impossible for the kids to hear what they were saying.

The conversation ended and Carlotta turned around. "It looks as if the stable's getting someone new," she called out. "Beth, please run to the tack room and get a rope."

"Okay!" The girl ran off and the driver lowered the ramp.

Curious, Ricki and the others moved in closer to take a look at the horse before it was even unloaded.

"Oh, he's cute!" gushed Lillian.

"But unbelievably thin," added Kevin.

"Get out of the way, kids," Carlotta firmly ordered them all aside, just as Beth returned and held out the rope.

136

Carlotta pointed at the trailer.

"Beth, please do me a favor and get that horse out of there. He'll be glad to have firm ground under his feet again. Oh, and you, young man," she turned to the driver, "please hand me those transport papers to sign."

The driver nodded, although it was clear that he wasn't happy about having a stranger unload the horse.

"Don't worry," Carlotta whispered to him. "Nothing's going to happen. Those two have known each other for a long time."

Beth went over to the trailer, but before she even set one foot on the ramp she turned white as a ghost and held her hand over her mouth so she wouldn't scream. Baffled, she took a step backward.

"What's wrong now?" asked Cathy, quietly. "Is there a horse in there, or a monster? Why's Beth freaking out?"

"Hurry up, child," Carlotta encouraged her with a smile. "How long do you want to let your Rondo stay in there?"

Nancy gave a start when she heard the horse's name. She glanced quickly at Warren, who winked at his wife and put his arm around her shoulder.

"You... *you* bought him back?"

Warren nodded.

"I don't know what to say," she whispered.

"Then don't say anything." He gave his wife a hug.

Beth was numb and standing in front of the trailer, staring at her horse.

I can't believe it! It can't be true, kept going through her head. She was afraid that it was just a dream.

Only when Rondo turned his head around and whinnied softly did she break out of her trance, and then nothing could hold her back.

She stepped up on the ramp, her knees shaking, and spoke soothingly to her horse, repeating his name over and over, incredulous. Rondo seemed to be instantly soothed by the sound of her voice, and he nudged her affectionately, as if in recognition.

Beth wrapped her arms around his neck and hugged him tightly.

"I'll never let you get away from me again, do you hear me? NEVER AGAIN! I swear it!"

* * *

Ricki and her friends looked at each with amazement when they heard Carlotta's words.

"I can't believe it," said Lillian, beaming. "She really got him back!"

"See, now we have proof that dreams really can come true," laughed Ricki. "And Carlotta never said a word!"

"She was probably afraid we couldn't keep a secret," responded Kevin. "This is really a fabulous surprise, Carlotta!" he called over to the ranch owner.

Carlotta just pointed at Warren Pendleton. "Yes, it is, but I don't deserve your praise. He does," she told the kids. Lillian's glance swept over to Beth's father.

"He doesn't seem that bad," Ricki whispered softly. "Beth made him out to be a real monster when she told us about him."

"Well, look," answered Kevin, whispering, "he did sell her horse, and that was definitely a lousy thing to do."

"But he also got him back, and I think he should win a few points with Beth for doing that... Oh, look at him... When Rondo gains a little weight, he's going to look fabulous!"

Beth led her horse off the ramp, and now she just stood there in the yard, a look of utter disbelief on her face.

Warren gave his wife another hug, and then he approached his daughter.

"Beth... " he began hesitatingly. "I'm so sorry I sold your horse. It was thoughtless of me not to consider your feelings in the matter. And I had no idea what the consequences would be for Rondo. He looks like a ghost of himself right now, and I know that's mostly my fault." He stopped talking a moment to wait for Beth's reaction, but she stayed silent.

"I hope the two of you can forgive me," he said, looking at Nancy, who came to his side. "I've been so wrapped up in the business and our relocating here, I haven't given any thought to the happiness of the two most important people in my life... but that's going to change."

Beth took a step forward, swallowed nervously, and wrapped her arms around her father and gave him a quick hug. "Thanks, Dad," she sniffed.

She jerked the long lead rope a little and her horse came two steps closer, too, so that he almost stepped on Warren's feet.

The animal looked at Beth's father with huge eyes,

stretched his neck trustingly, and blew his warm breath into the man's face. Warren smiled and stroked the gray horse gently over his forehead.

"I'm so sorry, gray man! But I promise you, I'll never do it again!" he said tenderly.

"All those promises are great," Carlotta said firmly, "but that horse needs some peace and quiet after his trip. I think we'll take him to the paddock so he can start getting acquainted with his stable mates right away."

"You want to put him with the others right away? Isn't that too dangerous?" asked Beth anxiously.

Carlotta smiled. "Don't worry, I'm not going to integrate Rondo into the herd today. Come with me." With these words, she turned and took off toward the paddocks.

"Let's see whom he gets along with best from the start!" Carlotta stopped and took the horse's lead rope from Beth and then led him to the paddock fence, where the other animals were already looking curiously at the new horse.

Carlotta and Rondo stood about three feet from the paddock. Old Jonah rumbled something to the gray Arabian. Somewhat nervous, Rondo took a step toward Jonah, and in a moment the two of them were rubbing their heads together.

"Okay, that's what I thought!" Carlotta indicated to Beth that she should take charge of her horse again, and then she went onto the paddock and led Jonah outside.

"We'll put the two of them on that little piece of meadow next to the paddock. They'll have their peace there and Rondo can get used to the others without being disturbed," explained Carlotta.

A few minutes later, the two horses were running next to one another, like old friends, and while they were closing the gate to the paddock, Rondo knelt down and rolled around luxuriously. It had been a long time since he had been outside on a meadow.

Beth was happy watching her horse. She stood at the fence for a long time that afternoon without taking her eyes off him, and she wished she could spend the night in the stable. Carlotta, however, gave her a firm NO, although she could understand the girl's desire very well.

"I'm still completely mixed up," Beth said to her friends as they went to get their bikes to go home.

"I can totally believe that, and now I can't wait for you to go riding with us, as soon as Rondo has recuperated a little!" said Ricki.

"With Carlotta taking care of him that won't take long," Kevin nodded.

"I think it's great that he's here!" Lillian patted the Arabian's neck.

"Well, he'll stay here until we find a good stall for him," answered Beth. "After all, he's not ready for retirement yet, even though he looks it right now."

"That's true! See you, Beth. We've got to get going. If it's not too late, we want to go riding this afternoon. We'll see you tomorrow at school!" Lillian winked at her new friend. "I hope you're not too excited to sleep tonight," she teased, and then she rode off with the others.

* * *

Carlotta went back into the house with the Pendletons.

"Since I'm definitely not going to sell my ranch, especially now that Rondo has my roof over his head, it would interest me to find out what's going to become of your plans to build a golf resort," she said lightly.

Pendleton looked at her thoughtfully and frowned. "Since your property is almost right in the middle of the planned site, it will be quite a problem to proceed with my plans," he said seriously. "The investors won't exactly be thrilled when I tell them that neither the hotel nor the golf course will be possible on this wonderful piece of land."

Carlotta sat down on her favorite chair and offered the Pendletons the couch.

"I don't really understand how it's possible to start the planning before one has made sure that the land will be available."

Warren smiled ironically. "In my experience, almost everything in this world is for sale, as long as the price is right."

"That's possible, but only *almost* everything." Carlotta nodded encouragingly. "And one should never underestimate, despite all that experience, the stubbornness of old women!"

Nancy Pendleton laughed out loud. "I think young women can be stubborn, too!" she said.

"Yes, but what's going to happen now with your plans?" Carlotta asked Warren again.

"Well, it's not as though we hadn't found an alternative property for the project," Pendleton admitted finally. "It's not nearly as ideal as the area around the fantastic Echo Lake, but it's definitely acceptable as far as location and size."

"There you are! That's what I thought!" Carlotta leaned back satisfied. "I was sure there was a Plan B."

"Of course, although the investors would have preferred this location!"

"Oh," Carlotta said, spontaneously. "If they want to invest in something here, then they should contribute to my planned riding hall."

Pendleton looked up. "You want to build a riding hall here? I didn't know anything about that."

"There's a lot you don't know," laughed Carlotta. "A small riding hall is almost a necessity; first of all, to give the animals enough exercise, even in winter, and secondly, so I can have guests in the cold months, when everything is frozen outside. The people who come here want to ride, obviously, and if it's icy outside it would be irresponsible to allow it. On the other hand, I have to have as many paying guests as possible throughout the year to be able to maintain the ranch. At the moment, I can only accept guests during the summer months."

Warren grinned. "My offer to buy the ranch is still open," he said, now that he was more aware of Carlotta's financial situation.

"No, no. Over my dead body! I just wanted to explain why I want to build a riding hall."

Nancy, who had listened closely, put her hand on her husband's arm.

"What do think, hon? Would it be possible to find someone who could invest some money in the riding hall project?"

Carlotta shook her head. "Hey, that was actually just a joke! I don't need any investors."

Pendleton looked thoughtfully at the two women. "Actually, that's not a bad idea. It's probably possible to find someone... the riding hall could be enlarged then, maybe a separate dorm could be built for more guests, the stable could be made bigger, and –"

"And then the whole spirit of Mercy Ranch would be ruined. I wouldn't have any say, and the money that came in would be filling someone's pockets instead of being used for my veterans." Carlotta objected immediately.

"It would just depend on the organization. The fact is, your financial situation would be much improved and you could hire some assistants that would help out. We should think this over again some time, Mrs. Mancini."

"Hmmm... maybe... but for the time being, I want to leave everything the way it is," Carlotta responded slowly. "However, if I change my mind, then I would be glad to reconsider your suggestions."

Pendleton nodded and then exchanged a look with his wife before they both got up to leave.

"We're going to go find Beth now," said Nancy, and held out her hand warmly to Carlotta. "Thanks for everything, and honestly, I like your Mercy Ranch here much better than a huge hotel."

"Well, at least you two are in agreement," laughed Warren, as the two left the house. He realized that he would have to rescind his offer to all of the farmers in the area, and that was going to be unpleasant, but meanwhile he could understand Carlotta's position. And if it weren't for her and her ranch, Rondo wouldn't have found a new home so quickly.

The most important thing is that Beth is happy again, and that our family is back together, the developer thought. Everything else was secondary for him now.

* * *

Cathy had been very quiet on the way home as Ricki, Lillian, and Kevin talked about Rondo and Beth. It was only now, as the friends rode their horses along Echo Lake on the trail through the woods, that Ricki noticed that her best friend hadn't said anything at all. She quickly urged Diablo on so that she could catch up to Cathy's dun.

"Hey, what's wrong? Aren't you happy for Beth?" she asked, although it suddenly became clear to her that that was the wrong question.

Cathy shrugged her shoulders.

"You guys have been talking nonstop about Beth! Rondo this, Rondo that... of course, I think it's great that she has her horse again, but, honestly, at the moment, I'm thinking more about my problem than about the Rondo problem, which has ceased to be a problem anyway."

Ricki felt guilty, and immediately decided to pay more attention to Cathy, the way a true girlfriend should.

"And what are you thinking about?" she asked with genuine interest.

"What do you think?"

Ricki sighed. "Hal."

"What else?" Cathy stared straight ahead, down the trail. "What did Carlotta say? Happiness takes strange paths. Sometimes it comes back to you indirectly, and sometimes it takes another form... It looks as if it's come back to Beth, and in my case, of course, it's completely too late."

"No way! It's not too late! You just have to be a little more patient. Not all guys are like Hal, and –"

"What's that supposed to mean?"

Ricki started to stammer. "Well, after all, he did ditch you for someone else, and –"

Cathy protested. "I've been thinking it over," she interrupted her friend. "Hal isn't a jerk! She, Lena, must have gotten to him, but don't ask me how."

Ricki would have liked to tell her that a guy who lets himself be influenced like that is definitely not the right guy for Cathy, but since she sensed that her friend still cared for Hal, she didn't say what she was thinking.

"You know what," Ricki said slowly. "I think it doesn't matter what I say, it would be the wrong thing. Still, Cathy, I think you should try to think about something else and let yourself be distracted."

The girl laughed. "If you could just tell me how I'm

supposed to do that, I would really appreciate it. You didn't think about anything else either, that time when Kevin was interested in someone else for a while, did you? You should be able to put yourself in my shoes!"

"I am, but it doesn't change anything when you keep mulling it over. If you keep going over and over it again and again, you'll make yourself crazy. I mean, of course, you can't get this out of your head. It'll probably stay in there for a long time. But do you want to stay this sad forever, and keep looking for an answer that no one can give you? Hal probably couldn't even give it to you himself!"

Cathy was silent, thinking over what Ricki had just said. Of course, she was right, and she would love to just stop thinking about her ex-boyfriend, but she didn't know how to do it.

"Hey, as soon as Rondo's fit, we have to go riding with Beth, here, around Echo Lake. After all, she dreamed about galloping along here on her horse!" called Lillian suddenly behind her.

Cathy started and felt a stab in her heart. Beth seemed to have really captured her friends' hearts quickly, and, in a way, it made her jealous. Would Rondo's owner manage to take away her friends, Ricki, Lillian, and Kevin? After all, she was the main topic with the kids, and they just wanted Cathy to get over her problem with Hal.

Cathy realized painfully, that she wouldn't be able to stand it if, after losing Hal, she also lost her friends. The more she thought about it the sadder she became.

I'm the only one in the group who doesn't have her own horse, she thought suddenly. *I'm always the outsider!* Even Beth, miraculously, got Rondo back, so she's in the same position now as the others.

Cathy continued her train of thought: *If she has a boyfriend some day, then I'll really be the fifth wheel! Man, they have no idea how terrible I feel, because I just don't fit in. I don't have my own horse… and I don't have a boyfriend.* Cathy couldn't stop thinking about how sad it all was. She even started to imagine that Beth would soon take her place in the group. *You're crazy!* she heard her inner voice say. *You won't lose your friends! On the contrary, you just made a new one!*

Cathy sighed and thought about it for a long time. "That's right!" she said out loud, smacking the side of her head with her palm. "I'm really an idiot!"

Ricki looked at her perplexed. "What do you mean?"

Cathy shook her head. "Nothing. I was just thinking out loud." she responded. When she saw the trail widen in front of her, leading out of the woods and across the meadows, it became clear that it was ridiculous to see the world through a veil of tears all the time, and predict things that would probably never happen anyway. There would always be wonderful moments in her life that were worth recognizing, and this moment was one of them.

"Do you guys have anything against a little gallop?" Cathy asked loudly, and smiled at Ricki. "I think I need it right now!"

Ricki grinned back.

"It's just what I've been waiting for!"

"Good idea," called voices from behind, and soon the rhythmical beating of the horses' hooves echoed in the woods.

* * *

Ricki sat lightly on her wonderful black horse. With each jump his long mane stroked her face and thousands of thoughts went through her mind, as always. But the thoughts flew away even faster than they arrived, and they lost their importance in view of the wonderful feeling that filled her at that moment.

What could be more wonderful than galloping with Diablo? With every step she left her problems behind her.

As Ricki sensed the powerful thrust of her horse beneath her, she felt incredibly strong, as if there was nothing that could upset or harm her. Diablo's energy seemed boundless, and it transferred to the girl whenever she allowed it.

How had she lived before the horse came into her life? Sometimes she couldn't remember what she had felt when she had ridden other horses. She had probably been extremely happy then, too, but her happiness now was beyond compare. What bound her to Diablo, whether she walked him through winter woods, galloped with him across mown meadows or just sat quietly with him in his stall and enjoyed being near him or watching him eat... These moments of familiarity and trust that existed between her and her horse, couldn't be compared with anything.

Diablo was there for her, no matter if she was in a good mood or if her heart was filled with sadness. As soon as she was near him, wrapping her arms around his strong neck or looking into his wise eyes, she knew that everything was going to be okay.

That is really amazing, Ricki thought at that moment, and it felt as though she were riding through a sea of emotions on her beloved horse. They were feelings that she would never have been able to describe with words, but nevertheless, they were in her heart.

She wondered if Cathy felt the same way on Rashid.

Sighing, she held Diablo back a little behind her friend's dun horse, as the riders approached the road. As always, she was sad that the ride couldn't last a little longer. But then, as Cathy turned around in her saddle, Ricki's sadness turned to joy. Her friend's eyes were as bright as always and a big smile lit her face.

"World, I'm back!" called out Cathy, as she leaned forward and rubbed Rashid between the ears. "Carlotta said that happiness sometimes comes back in another form, even though it seems as though it's left us. Well, you know what? I just realized that I never lost it. Even if Hal changes girlfriends a hundred times, I'll *still* have it... and better yet, my happiness even has a name!" She pointed to her horse. "Rashid!"